I0677651

ROAD WORK

Jeff Bender

© 2019 Lulu Author. All rights reserved.
ISBN 978–0–9832512–2–4

I take with me where I go
A pen and a golden bowl.
Poet and beggar step in my shoes
Or a prince in a purple shawl.

I bring with me when I return
To the house that my father's hands made,
A crooning bird on a crystal bough
And oh, a sad, sad word.

An old Welsh folk song

GRAPES OF WRATH

Woody Guthrie sings gray songs that rise to the shimmering edge of the atmosphere. Clouds flow from fixed nostalgia-streams of ancestral memory. God's tongue grooms the earth for dangerous greatness, like a mother cat tending to her young. The light is so thick that I touch it and smooth its physics-fur to the glass flesh of the waiting spring. I move through reluctant mornings, gathering ripe fruits and berries from thorny vines. Pastel petals fall and shatter the howling silence.

This tortured dust is my cellmate, condemned to the same parched prison as the earth. Homeless farm families seek elusive crops to pick, clinging to the great motherland that is at once their clear birth, death and bare existence in purple valleys of proud and defiant mountains and wilting trees. Reflections in the mirrored walls of my skull glitter like chrome handles of old vending machine candy calling to me through the posted glass.

"Them's two fer a penny," the waitress said, as she placed the sticks of candy in the children's hands. The truck drivers teased her soft heart over their coffee.

"Hey, those ain't two fer a penny, they're a nickel a piece." one of drivers said.

"What's it to ya?" she replied, eyes open to highways' tempting illusions of just one last run.

"Hey! Wait a minute! You got change!" she shouted, as the drivers tossed her their money and walked through the door.

"What's it to ya!" one snapped back, smiling in a tender-tough gesture that stretched like a late afternoon shadow across the truck stop myth of America.

DANE

I am five years old. I live in Dane, West Virginia with my father, mother and baby sister. We live in a four room little house on a main road beside a gas station. The front door of our house is one step up. We have no porch, just a little stoop at the front door. There is a loose wire fence around the front lawn to keep me from wandering into the road. I play there during the day. I spend much of my time watching cars that come and go at the gas station. There is always something interesting going on there.

Once I saw a car speed into the station. Before it reached the pumps though, a boy on the passenger's side threw open the door and jumped out while the car was still moving. He ran right up to the fence where I was standing. He was laughing. He looked at me and laughed again. He was wearing a white T-shirt and blue jeans with a thick black belt. The big gold buckle of the belt was cocked off to the side. He had long wavy blond hair combed back from his face. He smiled then turned and walked back to the car, which had stopped and parked at the pumps.

A young boy lived next door to us. He is older than I am, maybe eight or twelve. He is nice. Sometimes he comes over to play. We play catch with my big rubber ball, or tag or hide and seek. One day he came over and we ran around for a while. We played tag and catch with my ball, then he suggested that we go to his house to play. My mother gave her permission. We explored the edge of the woods in his back yard for a while, and then he said, "Let's go into my basement to play." I agreed and followed him. When we reached the basement, he unzipped his pants and pulled his wee-wee out. It was big and stiff.

7

I looked at it. "Suck it." he said. He was my friend so I did. It tasted like a big salty thumb.

A SNAKE DANCE

My family migrated from Craigsville, West Virginia to Medina Ohio, a small town about thirty miles south of Cleveland, when I was five years old. And every summer after that we went back to West Virginia to visit our relatives. We stayed at my Granddad's little farm. My cousins lived next door. We chased chickens and played baseball, tag and other summer games all day. We ran through the ancient woods that expanded in a leafy mystery behind my cousin's house. We played soldier and cowboy games there, through long sunny afternoons. The trees were thick and dark in the woods. We spent hours exploring slow flowing streams and the soft forest floor. It was always cool and damp there, because it seemed to rain in West Virginia, at least a little bit, every day. Sometimes it rained all day but the rain was different there than it was Ohio. Warm heavy droplets penetrated our bodies and cooled our young souls, when we took off our shirts and ran through the downpour.

We were playing four-way catch on one of those hot shirtless days in Larry's back yard. The yard was long and narrow but flat between the gray weatherworn tool shed and the long back porch of the house. We positioned ourselves in the shape of a narrow diamond and played four-way catch for what seemed like hours. Larry and Shawn were a year or two younger than Stan and me. Larry and Stan were the best players but I was better than Shawn. Larry had short, coarse brown hair and a scattering of freckles across his cheeks and nose. Stan and Shawn had blond hair, but Stan's was cut in a flattop and Shawn's was long. We were all gangly and tan. One day, giant white mountains of clouds floated in the sky as we played in the sun, then a sudden summer rainstorm blew up in the early afternoon. It started about twenty feet away from us as we played catch in the sun. We were thrilled by this seeming miracle and ran around the yard in tickling laughter, trying to escape the thick drops, as the sheeting wall of water rushed our way.

A damp musty smell always lingered in the woods. A path behind the shed led through a fairyland canopy of leaves. In the woods, we became hunters, explorers or pioneers taming a savage wilderness. One of our favorite pastimes was hunting for snakes. Water moccasins and rattlesnakes thrived in the area so we had to be careful. The snakes weren't a problem for us though, because in our cautious little minds every snake we saw was a Moccasin or Rattler. If they were too big or had remarkably colorful stripes or designs on their bodies, we were sure they were poisonous and wouldn't touch them. The toothless little garter snakes were harmless enough though, so they became our chosen prey. We loved it when we caught one and it bit our hands with its pinching little mouth as it tried to crawl away; but we only allowed them to crawl from hand to hand, cousin to cousin, in an endless illusion of escape.

I was nine or ten years old when I caught my last snake. We found it in the woods a little after lunch and played with it until mid-afternoon. We made it crawl through the jagged opening of a rusty tin can we found in the woods. It wouldn't crawl in on its own, so we pushed it in until it did. It crawled slowly and carefully. "Look!" Stan said, "It hurts its skin."

We took the snake back to the house and made it crawl across the gravel driveway, to see if that would hurt it too. Dust caked its slithering little belly. Larry said, "Let's make it crawl across the road!"

and the rest of us agreed. We placed the snake at the side of the two-lane highway that ran in front of Granddad's house, then pushed it out with a stick. The temperature was in the eighties or nineties. Blacktop tar was soft and runny in the heat. The snake tried to turn back but we pushed it out until it crawled on its own. A few cars flew by and just missed the snake. "Go snake! You can make it!" we screamed.

It almost reached the middle of the road, when the pick-up truck blew by and caught it right in the middle of its body. When the tire hit, the snake's head stretched up. It's toothless little mouth was wide open, like its jaw-bones weren't even attached, as it helplessly struck at the tire like a vicious little rattler. As fast as the tire hit though, it was gone. The snake was still alive and wiggling but couldn't crawl away. The center of its body was smashed in the road. Two other cars hit it after that, and it became a skinny stain on the pavement, which remained for the rest of our visit. I looked at it every day. The last time I saw it one was when we pulled out of the driveway and headed home. I stared at it as we left, and its' image became forever imbedded in my soul.

CORNBREAD AND BEANS

Craigsville

My Granddad had a little farm in Craigsville, West Virginia; a small crossroads town nestled in the Allegheny Mountains about a hundred miles east of Charleston and fifty miles west of the Virginia border. Granddad and Grandma had fourteen children, ten boys and four girls, but the youngest boy died as a baby. The farm provided the family with much of the food they needed and a little income. They had a cow for milk. They raised corn, tomatoes, potatoes, carrots, cabbage and greens; chickens for eggs and cooking, and pigs for bacon and pork. The boys' jobs were to do the farm chores and run the place while Granddad managed his little general store or coal mine. Three of the four girls had to quit school in the eighth grade; to help Grandma clean, wash, cook and serve the boys at mealtime. The girls ate when the boys finished. Grandma made cornbread and beans, because it was such a cheap and healthy meal for her strapping farm-boy hoard. "It fills 'em up and keeps 'em goin'," she said.

There's no better food in the world than cornbread and beans. Any kind of beans will do; navy, red, brown, pinto or kidney. Grandma made the best cornbread and beans. No store-bought bread or canned beans for her; she made it all from scratch. Dried beans were soaked and slow-cooked all morning, while the cornmeal batter was mixed and baked to golden perfection with a firm brown bakery edge.

When I was little, Grandma still made cornbread and beans, though her family was gone; and after supper I'd sit with Granddad while my mom helped clear the table and do the dishes. Granddad would slice a chunk of cornbread in half, butter the halves and give one to me. We dipped the corn bread into the soupy bean juice at the bottom of the serving bowl and ate as we talked.

Grandma's whole life was focused on preparing meals for her family. Huge feasts were served three times a day. She made mounds of ham, bacon and eggs or buttermilk pancakes for breakfast. The noon meal was as big as a steamy evening supper; corn, potatoes, beans and pork were spread on the dining table for the boys when they came in from the fields. Supper was the same as lunch; only different meat, potatoes and vegetables, and if she didn't make cornbread, the meals came with a never-ending supply of warm flaky biscuits.

Later on, Grandma did odd things in the kitchen, like putting salt in the buttermilk pancakes instead of sugar. No one said anything; she cried when she didn't get it right. After her stroke, she never cooked again.

Grandma Blake

I am nine years old. Grandma rocks a baby doll in the living room. She rocks pictures of babies she finds in magazines too. Her long white hair is pinned in a tight bun at the back of her head. Unpinned, it hangs like a waterfall down her back. "She always loved to rock the babies," my mother says, "she rocked all of her children and grandchildren. She rocked you too. Don't you remember?" I don't remember but Grandma's lap looks soft and comfortable. She holds the doll close to her sagging breasts and sings to her baby as she rocks.

I am sixteen; *Wildwood Flower*, by Joan Baez is one of my favorite songs. I play it over and over again. I love the way the longing words and music burrow into my soul. I play it for my mom. When the song finishes, she says, "Your Grandma used to gather all us

14

kids together and sing that song when we were little. She loved The Carter Family."

My mother told other stories about Grandma. I see her running from bulls through short cuts across fields on her way home from school. She rides a horse, bareback, skirt thigh-high over rolling West Virginia fields glowing with asters, black-eyed Susans and goldenrod swaying in the late summer air. Sweet earth-smells of dirt and clay mix with the scents of grass and weeds. She rides, leaning forward into the horse's sweaty shoulders. Her knees grip the horse's heaving ribs as her long hair flaps like a torn blonde flag in the wind. Galloping hooves keep time with the wildwood beat of her heart.

The Promised Land

An old clock ticked on the living room wall of Granddad's house. It had a big round face, yellowed with age, with Roman Numerals for numbers. The face had a glass cover that opened on little brass hinges, so the hands could be set and the clock could be wound with its big brass key. Granddad wound it every day. The clock was dark-stained hardwood. A small beveled-glass window revealed the short brass pendulum swinging beneath the face. The ticking of the clock was the background noise for everything that happened in the house, click-clock, click-clock, especially when it was quiet.

I was ten or eleven years old on the December day that Grandma died, excused from school to go to the funeral. Grandma was laid out in an open casket in the living room. She looked like she was sleeping but her skin was clay-gray, so I knew better. The clock was stopped. Its hands pointed to the time of Grandma's death. I heard my aunts and uncles talking about it. "It's a miracle," somebody said.

15

"The clock stopped right when she died." Later, I found out that Granddad had stopped the clock and positioned the hands at the time of Grandma's death according to an old custom. Granddad was peaceful, a religious man, an elder in the church. He had a fundamental way of dealing with life and death.

All of Grandma's children came to the funeral, from towns all over the country, grown up with families of their own. They brought a mob of grandchildren and great grandchildren with them. There were many cousins I didn't know. It was a cold day, sunny, no snow but a bitter wind blew. Kind words were said; then the preacher blessed Grandma and sent her on her way. After the funeral, we all went back to the house for conversation and consolation; and to share our memories of her over a table filled with steaming platters and bowls of food, including cornbread and beans, prepared by her daughters.

MAN LEGS

I just spent the last two weeks in mental and physical agony, and I still can't fix the shifting lever on my truck. I've taken it apart and put it together again so many times I could do it in the dark, using my sensory mechanical memory to complete the job. I don't understand. Every time I reassemble the steering column; with all of the tubes, bolts, washers, gaskets and other unnamed gadgets lined up and properly attached to the front axle, I never have enough room left on the column for the steering wheel. When I finish, there is only about half of a thread left on the main shaft to screw on the last nut. I can't even get the nut started.

I have never been good with machines though. I don't understand them. They are too linear and logical for my ethereal mind to comprehend. So, whenever I try to fix one, I end up bashing my knuckles on cold hard steel, and smearing black grease into my torn and bloody skin. Then, about half way through the job, I discover that I don't have the proper tools or knowledge to complete it. So, I have developed a number of coping skills to help me work around my mechanical dilemmas; and sometimes my ignorance paid off, like that summer my boy-legs became the legs of a man.

I had a three-speed English racing bike that was stuck in third gear and I couldn't fix it. All of my friends could fix their bikes, but I never figured it out so I lived with it and rode it the way it was. It was hard to pedal. I managed though; pumping my puny piston legs, fired by the watered down fuel of my weight interacting with gravity, and my desire to attain cruising speed through long boyhood afternoons. I strained against the heavy resistance of the mechanical power train

17

floating beneath me, grinding that fat sprocket in slow motion around third gear, on a sacred quest calling me to swimming pool and baseball adventures in laughter.

Dave was my best friend, but he didn't have a bike that summer. His bike was broken or stolen or too small for him, maybe it just needed a new tire, I can't remember. Anyway, he had no wheels, so I pedaled him around town when we played. He sat sidesaddle on the crossbar between the handlebars and the seat. I didn't mind. He was my friend. I didn't even think about how hard it was; I just did it.

Over the summer, my calves and thighs grew into hard little balls bulging slightly under my hairless twelve-year-old skin, and the boy legs that had so faithfully carried my beanpole body around for all those years, disappeared. As the summer passed, the pedaling became easier. By the end of the summer my legs were full, firm and strong. And, without knowing it, I had pedaled my into the indifferent mysteries of manhood; and the ever evolving, disposable nature of male understanding. Dave and my third gear had propelled me to a place from which I could never return. So, I gather up my tools to attempt another shifting lever repair and wonder if anything important will happen this time.

THE DEER

Mike and I spent long days together in the woods when we were kids; on backpack journeys through golden seasons, tracking wildlife and careless boyhood joy. We caught frogs and snakes and took them home. In season, we hunted rabbits and squirrels. The last time I saw Mike was the summer after our high school graduation. He was tall, lean, athletic and strong; with dark brown hair cut in a flattop. His eyes were blue-gray like a wolf. Mike had his new lever action 30-30, a graduation gift from his dad. I had my .22. We packed a few sandwiches, and we each had a canteen of water. The sky overflowed with gray-white mountains of clouds. A gentle breeze fanned our sweating faces and fluttered the leaves around us as we walked. Birds, squirrels and chipmunks chittered and scurried. Sticks and dry leaves crackled under our feet. Sweet damp forest smells filled the air. The path we followed was overgrown and rarely used. We left it and climbed a small rise on the right, then stopped to rest in a cluster of pines at the top.

Just over the rise was a pond. Tall, thick, yellow-green clusters of grass and stiff brown cattails stood proud along the bank. The opposite bank was thick with trees growing close to the edge of the water. Mosquitoes, bees and dragonflies buzzed. Frogs and birds were calling. We found a spot to rest and took off our gear. An old oak tree shaded the area. Patches of sunlight broke through the leaves and danced around us when the wind blew. I found a place to sit, lit a cigarette, took a drink from my canteen and stared at the pond. Mike stood up and pulled out his knife. It was about a foot long with a carved ivory handle. The blade spread wide in a thick sharp curve. He threw the knife at a fallen tree trunk about fifteen feet away, retrieved it and threw it again. He threw it often, for long periods of time. He loved to stick things.

One summer day, when we were kids, Mike found some green metal tent stakes in his father's garage. The stakes were about fourteen inches long. Mike decided that they were frog spears. So, we each grabbed one and headed to a creek behind a church where we played. When we approached, frogs were sitting and croaking along the bank, and didn't jump away when we walked up, mating time maybe. Mike took advantage of the easy prey and stabbed the frogs where they sat. His eyes were wide and wild; like he was trying to see through each frog's skin as his spear pierced their leathery little bodies. My stomach tightened. I couldn't bring myself to stab one; and every time Mike stabbed, I heard a dull puncturing "THUCK" that made me shiver. Frogs bodies floated in the water and Mike kept stabbing, like a mad scientist priest performing some ritual frog experiment.

I picked up Mike's new rifle. It had a smooth walnut stock and handgrip that ran half way under the deep blue barrel. It was heavier than my .22 but felt good in my hands. It was a graduation gift from his dad. His dad always gave Mike expensive gifts, and Mike always had a fat wad of money in his pocket too. Whenever we went out, he bought cokes, fries, shakes and records for me. In return, I did what he wanted to do. We were getting ready to go out at Mike's house one day, and Mike thought he needed some more money; so he robbed his invalid grandmother. Mike's family took care of her, but to Mike she was just old and in the way; and served no useful purpose except as an easy source of cash. She had a habit of stashing money around the house in secret places. Mike found her hiding spots and pilfered her money whenever he could. When we walked downstairs, his Grandmother was hobbling through the living room.

"Get to your room you stupid bitch!" Mike yelled. She started to say something but Mike screamed again. "I said move!" She turned and hobbled off as Mike fumbled through her purse.

I examined his new rifle, "Ya wanna shoot it?" he said.

"Sure, what'll we shoot?"

He looked around, "How about that log over there?" I looked to where he pointed and saw a fallen tree about twenty yards away. He sheathed his knife, grabbed the rifle, reached into his backpack for bullets, loaded the gun, cocked it and handed it to me. I raised it to my shoulder, rested my elbows on my knees, sighted in the log and squeezed the trigger. When the gun fired the recoil hit me like a fist. Mud exploded high and to the right behind the log. I groaned and grabbed my shoulder. Mike grabbed the rifle and grinned as I rubbed my pain away.

"Okay smart ass!" I said. "You hit it!"

Mike was standing. "Ya gotta pull it tight ta y'r shoulder," he said. Then he cocked the gun, brought it up, aimed and fired. A piece of the log chipped off near the end. "Shit!" he said, "I was aimin' at that that branch stickin' up there. Somethin's wrong with this fuckin' gun! It ain't sighted in right!"

"Take it easy man! You'll hit it!" I replied. He cocked the rifle, fired another round and missed again. We took turns shooting at the branch. I tried to adjust my aim but never came close to hitting it. Mike got closer than I did, but he missed too; and the more he missed, the madder he got. I stopped shooting, lit a smoke and watched the ripples dancing on the pond in the afternoon light. Mike stopped shooting a little later. He pulled out a couple of beers from his backpack and handed one to me. We drank in silence. We took a few more shots and drank two more beers. Mike kept shooting but could never hit the branch. He sat down again, wrapped his arms around his knees and stared at the ground, rocking slightly and mumbling to himself. I didn't say anything. I'd seen him like that before. It was best to leave him alone. He stood up and wandered into the trees with the rifle slung over his shoulder. I stretched out on the grass and dozed off.

When I woke up, the sun was gone. A cool breeze blew through the trees and the sky was charcoal gray. A storm was brewing. I gathered my gear. As I worked, I saw something move in the trees about fifty yards away. A doe stepped into the clearing. She moved cautiously toward the pond. When she reached the water she drank, lifting her head occasionally to look around. I stood still, trying to blend in with the forest to watch her.

A rifle crack ruptured the silence. The doe's hind-legs collapsed and she sat on the bank like a stubborn mule. She struggled to her feet and was hobbling toward the trees when the second shot cracked. The blast cut through me like an electric jolt. The doe fell again, kicking in the grass, but she couldn't get back up. Mike stepped from behind a tree about thirty yards away and ran toward the deer. I was up and running too. He reached her before I did, and was standing over her when I arrived. The doe was still alive but her breath was thick, strained and gasping. Blood oozed from wounds in her mid and hind section. I was curious, excited and angry all at once. She watched us with huge brown eyes as she struggled. "What the hell are you doin?" I screamed.

Mike stared at her. His eyes were wild. His face beamed as he panted. "I just wanted ta see if I could hit 'er, you know. Not bad, right?"

"Not bad? You asshole! Finish 'er off!"

"Okay! Okay! Take it easy man! Relax! She'll be dead in a minute." He knelt down, pulled out his knife and stabbed the deer in the side. "Thuck. Thuck. Thuck." The doe jerked with every thrust.

"Kill 'er, you son-of-a-bitch!" I screamed.

"What's y'r problem?" he said, "She'll be dead in a minute." Then he stabbed her in the neck and drew the knife across her sleek throat. Blood flowed out and into a dark red pool in the grass. A light rain began to fall, almost a mist. The doe stopped moving. "Let's get outta here." he said.

When he turned to leave, something snapped in me and I drove my fist into his stomach. He dropped the knife and rifle, doubled over, then looked up. His eyes were wild. His mouth was contorted and snarling. His lips were rolled back. He lunged at me like a linebacker. We fell to the ground, wrestling, kicking and grabbing. Mike was stronger than I was. He worked his arms around my waist and squeezed. I thought my ribs would cave in. I couldn't breathe. I struggled to break loose, swinging my fists, but he wouldn't let go. He rolled on top of me and worked one arm around my head; then smashed me in the face with his free fist in a blind red rage. Pain radiated from my mouth and nose. I closed my eyes and blacked out.

When I came to, Mike was gone. My ribs ached. My face throbbed. My nose was broken; I could tell by the way I could wiggle it around my face. My two front teeth were smashed in too. I rubbed my tongue over them. They were pushed back against the roof of my mouth. I worked my thumb in behind and jerked them out straight again. Pain shot through my head like a twelve-volt slap. I shook it off and got to my feet. A heavy rain was falling. The blood under the doe's head looked like a red plastic pillow in the wet matted grass. Her huge dark eye stared out at nothing. I picked up my things and walked back to town.

I didn't see Mike for the rest of that summer. My nose was broken, along with two of my ribs. I ended up loosing one of my front teeth. My parent's were furious. "You're paying for this!" They said, "That's what you get for fighting!"

I headed off to college in September but didn't want to be there. I drank, partied and flunked out at Christmas. I married Louise when she got pregnant, and found a factory job in Cleveland. I worked all day and drank all night. Ten years later, Louise took the kids and ran off with a truck driver from Oklahoma. "He wants to take care of me!" her note said, "He loves me and I'm tired of being alone!"

Mike dropped out of college in his second year and enlisted in the Marines. He went to Vietnam, re-enlisted for three tours of duty and came home a hero with a Medal of Honor and a steel plate in his head for his valor. The local paper ran the story. A company of North Vietnamese soldiers overran Mike's firebase and managed to breach the perimeter defenses. The fighting took place inside the compound. Bodies of wounded, broken and dead American and South Vietnamese soldiers littered the ground. Mike was shot three times; once in the head, but he never quit. He counter-attacked; running from body to body, picking up rifles and machine guns of his fallen companions as he ran, and empting them on the enemy. Then, he scrambled to another body for another gun. He emptied clip after clip on the invaders, relentless in his pursuit. He killed mercilessly, on instinct, without hesitation, oblivious to his own pain and void of any remorse or mercy. The paper said he saved many of his buddies' lives, and single-handedly held off the enemy until the remaining troops could regroup and drive back the attack.

I am an inventory clerk in the Ford factory during the day, and spend my nights on a barstool in The Gutter Ball bar behind the bowling ally; staring at myself in the mirror behind the bar and exercising my right arm, lifting my drinks to get ready for the next game.

BACK ROADS

Mad motor hot-rods scream down this high school highway get-a-way night with Bob in his parents' new Pontiac station wagon, a big engine road rocket with well padded seats. Smokey and the Miracles moan "The Tracks of my Tears" on the radio. We stop at The Big Clown drive-in outside of town for some burgers, fries and shakes. "Louie, Louie" blares from the radio.

Then Joe, my girl's ex-boyfriend, sees us and chases us down a back country road in his friend's muscle-motor Grand Prix, in a rage of teenage love. I don't want Joe to catch us. He beat up the meanest hood in school and left him twitching in a pool of blood, a red blob lying like road kill at the side of some Podunk road. Joe sat on the guy and grabbed him by his long blonde DA wings, then started smashing his head against the pavement. Joe's friends had to pull Joe off before he killed the guy. Bob's left arm rests on the open window. I control the radio, Buddy Holly sings, "Not Fade Away." I crank it up. Bob steers with his right hand. With his blonde crew cut and rolled up tee-shirt sleeves, he looks like a like a high school greaser with a cigarette clenched in his teeth, going a hundred miles an hour with Joe and his buddy right on our tail; cursing, head-long at a hundred miles an hour, with Joe and his buddy right on our tail, into a dead-end "T" in the road flying right at us.

Bob doesn't slow down a bit when he hits that "T"; he just locks up the breaks and cuts the wheel to the left, like Steve Mc Queen sliding on a dime into that ninety-degree direction we were seeking. He cuts the wheel too far though, and we spin three doughnuts across some farmer's front lawn. Joe and his buddy bounce right by. Bob turns to the right and the Grand Prix just misses the rear end of the wagon spinning out of the way, in an automotive greaser-ballet that could not have been choreographed any better.

Turning to a stop, the nose of the Pontiac points down the same road we just came in on. "She's real fine my 409" The Beach boys sing from the radio, along with the hum of the engine, which is still running. So Bob peels out across the lawn and back down the same road we just came in on, the final lap of our great escape.

THE PARTY

Phil and I headed out in his tu-tone, red and white, '57 Chevy to a party at Debby's house on a warm spring Saturday night. We knew Debby but didn't hang out in her crowd. She was cute, tall and thin; a middle-class pre-sorority girl with professionally styled shoulder length brown hair. She was wearing a pastel pink sleeveless top, Bermuda shorts and white sneakers. It was spring and school was almost over. All of the kids would be there, invited or not. Phil and I didn't know where Debby's house was, but we knew the name of the street where she lived. When we neared her house though, cars lined both sides of the street and music blared from the basement of a split-level suburban duplex; so we knew that we found right place. Kids were running in and out of the basement family room as we walked in. They danced and talked, shoulder to shoulder. Rock an' Roll rhythms blared from the stereo. Some kids were smokin' and snacks were floatin' around.

Phil said, "This place needs a boost. Let's get some booze."

"What're ya talkin' about? How?" I said, "You got an I.D.?"

"No, I don't need one. I know how to get into the Forest Hills Country Club, and I know where they keep it. Watta ya say?"

"Let's go!" I said.

We climbed into the Chevy and took off. When we got there, he pulled into the country club and parked at the side of the road in some bushes. We got out and he whispered, "Follow me." We crouched low and cut across the field. Phil led me to a basement window that he knew was always open. He wiggled in and I followed. "Come on!" he said. "It's over here."

I crawled through and we grabbed eight or so half-filled bottles, then I climbed back out first and Phil passed the bottles up to me, then he crawled out. We carried the booze to the car, Phil fired up the Chevy and we headed back to the party. When we got there, he parked the car and we each grabbed a couple of bottles, then headed to the basement. Kids were laughing, screaming and running around the lawn as we approached; some kids were running around the neighborhood. We ran into Allen on the way in. He was hurrying out. "What's goin' on?" Phil asked, "This is nuts!"

"I know!" Allen replied, "It ain't good! Somebody snuck some beer in. Big Jeff was poundin' 'em down like crazy an' got mean; pushin' people around an' threatenin' everybody. Debbie's parents are upstairs. They're bound to pick up on what's goin' on. I'm gettin' outta here before they do. I don't want no trouble! See ya later!"

Debbie ran up; tears streamed down her red cheeks; her neatly styled hair was a mess, "Get that stuff outta here!" she screamed, "Go! Just go!"

"Okay! Okay!" I said. "You're right! We'll go!" We took off and cruised around town for a while, looking for a place to drink in peace; then I spotted Sue, my ex-girlfriend, walking down the street with a few of her friends. "Pull over man!" I said, "Stop!"

"Why?"

"Pick up Sue. She loves to party an' she might know someplace ta go. It'll be fun." Phil pulled over and stopped. I rolled down the window and yelled, "Hey, Sue, how ya doin'?"

She walked over. "I'm okay. How 'bout you?"

"I'm good! Listen, we got some booze. Wanna help us drink it?"

"You bet!" she said. She bid her friends goodbye and climbed into the front seat between us. We drove around for a while, then Phil pulled into Dog 'n Suds, a hot dog and root beer drive-in on the outskirts of town. Marty and Jeff were there too. We parked next to them and they joined us. Big Jeff was sober again and had returned to his "Big Dumb" self, so it seemed okay but we still had nowhere to go. "We can go to my parent's summer camp on Chippewa Lake if ya want to?" Sue said. "I don't have a key but I know how to get in." We agreed and took off.

The camp was nestled on a spider-leg dirt road that ran through a cluster of other camps along the shore. We found Sue's parent's camp and parked. Sue crawled through a small window and unlocked the door. The cabin was bare, except for a few white wicker chairs and a warped white rocking chair. Pictures of the lake and family hung in bamboo frames on the paneled walls. The floors were covered with worn, gray-pink flower-printed linoleum. There were three or four bedrooms in the place; each with a brown, metal-framed double bed with a lumpy mattress under a thin cotton bedspread. A worn wooden counter and stained porcelain sink, refrigerator and gas stove served as a corner kitchen. It was a cozy little place; but cold, musty and closed in. We sat in a circle on the floor of the living room and drank shots of whisky.

"Try this one, it's good!" someone would say, or "Let me have another hit o' that one!" We mixed and matched the booze; a shot o' Bourbon then Vodka, then a shot o' Gin. It all tasted like kerosene or rocket fuel to me, but it made me feel good. We talked and laughed;

31

and the more we laughed, the louder our voices vibrated in my ears. I poured another shot but missed the glass. Whisky spilled on the floor. I poured again but the glass kept moving. I looked up and discovered that the whole room was tipping. My friends were blurry and melting. I tried to get up but fell down. Someone said something I couldn't make it out. The voice blended with all the other screaming voices throbbing vibrations in my skull. Then, out of nowhere, Sue was in my face, "Stand up baby," she said, "I'll help ya."

The slow motion drone of her words fascinated me. I forgot why I wanted to get up. Sue stood up and pulled my arm. I didn't know why she was pulling it but I tried to stand to please her. I fell again, taking her with me. Phil appeared. I couldn't believe how well he could stand in that tilting room. He pulled me to my feet. The room spun faster. I felt sick and headed for the bathroom. I staggered in and fell, but Sue and Phil grabbed me. "I gotta throw-up," I said.

Big Jeff appeared. He was in my face, nose to nose, screaming about something. He pushed me into the bathroom. I fell down and threw-up on the floor. Sue helped me to the toilet where I began an all-night ritual purging of guts and alcohol. I was either lying on the floor of the bathroom or hanging my head over the toilet, kneeling in vomit, or spinning on a bed. Big Jeff appeared in my dreams, engaged in angry screaming; pushing me and shoving me around. Phil and Marty were stumbling around, trying to hold him back and calm him down. Then, he'd reappear; screaming and throwing me around again, in a timeless blur that finally came into focus at dawn.

I was still half drunk and sick when I came to. My throat was raw and burning and my stomach muscles ached. I was dizzy and nauseous. It was Sunday morning and I had to get to work. The cabin was destroyed. The floors were wet with whisky and puke. Chairs and tables were tipped over, and dishes and glasses were broken on the floor. The bedrooms were in shambles too; blankets and bedding were strewn everywhere. A stench of teenage alcohol schemes filled the chilly morning air. Phil drove me home but we didn't talk, and I didn't know or care about what happened to everyone else. My parents were awake and getting ready in their room for a trip to Cleveland when I walked in. I headed straight to the bathroom for a shower before they saw me. I was in the shower when my mother called through the door. "We're leaving now. We won't be back 'til late." She said.

"Okay. Bye. Have a good trip." I replied.

I shaved, dressed and headed to work. I was still dizzy and nauseous but climbed into my car and took off. I was a carhop at The Big Clown Drive In. The place specialized in burgers, hot dogs, cokes, fries and shakes; and was patronized by high school kids and hot rod heroes cruising for drag-race action outside of town. I had worked there for about six months. My boss, Larry, and his wife, Marsha, were young, friendly and ambitious. They hired high school boys to work as car hops, because high school students were their biggest customers. We wore white shirts, black bow ties and black pants, and black nylon windbreakers at night, if it was chilly. Larry insisted that we show up for our shifts on time. He was a nice guy and forgave many of our teenage faults; but his main goal was to make sure that his restaurant succeeded.

I made it to work, but was still a little groggy; my stomach wrenched and my head pounded. It was ten o'clock on a Sunday morning, a slow day anyway; so I figured that it wouldn't get busy until about noon. I had a burger, fries and a chocolate shake for breakfast, to settle my stomach, then a car pulled in. I walked out to take their order. "We'll have two Big Clown's, a large order of fries and two Cokes." The driver said.

"It'll be about ten minutes." I replied, then headed back to the building. My stomach gurgled and erupted as I walked. Puke shot from my gut but I caught it and held it in my mouth so I wouldn't scare the customers away. When I reached the bathroom, I spit it out. *If I can just hang on for the morning, I'll be okay by lunch.* I thought.

The cops showed up and arrested me around eleven o'clock. A state trooper and a city cop arrived in the trooper's car. Larry spoke to them, "Please! Let him finish his shift! I'll bring him in when he's done!"

"Sorry sir," the deputy said, "can't do that." Then he cuffed me, shoved me into the back seat of the car and took me away. They drove around the city park on the way to the jail, so the community see which criminal they had apprehended. I spent a week there with Phil, Tony and Kurt.

Tony and Kurt had attended Debby's party also then decided brake into the high school. They knew about a filing cabinet in the industrial arts room that contained money. They pried open a window and carried the cabinet out of the building to the parking lot, then tried to force it open with a hammer and screwdriver but couldn't, so they left it and ran. Somehow the police found out that they had done it; someone squealed or talked about it, so the police picked them up. We spent a week in jail together, and had our trials were held in back-to-back cases. The judge asked each of us to explain in detail what we had done. We explained. He asked questions about how and why we had done it. We answered. My mother cried as I told my story. We

34

were all found guilty and put on probation for three months. It was a big story in the local paper. I was kicked off of the tennis team, girls were not permitted to go out with me, and old friends were hard to find.

PAT'S PLACE

John and Jackie had been visiting their parents and friends in Ohio for about five months; but were headed back to Oregon with their sons, Michael and Dylan. My wife and I, along our two kids and friends, Dee and Ken, escorted them as far as Pat's Place; an old schoolhouse located on the Michigan side of the Ohio border, a few miles north of Toledo. Rick, Jerry and Pete lived there with Pat, and shared the expenses; but Pat was the driving force of the group and the head cook. They had converted the schoolhouse into a Whole Earth Catalog, natural-organic, psychedelic, back-to-the-land bunkhouse. The inside of the building was a huge open space with high ceilings; so the guys built their beds on lengths of weather-eaten fence posts, to take advantage of the rising heat when nights were cold. The spaces under their beds were used for closets and storage. They had erected barn-board partitions that formed little rooms around their beds. When we arrived, they had a full house for the weekend, so a party was in order; feasting, music, dancing, flower power, free love and nickel beer.

John and Jackie

John was a tall blonde artist of Scandinavian descent. He wore wire-rimmed glasses that he glared through like an anarchist from an old Russian novel. He had a gentle street-wise spirit and alert imagination. Jackie, his wife, was a little brunette with a tight body. Her posture was straight and proud with hard little breasts that were always thrust out, forming an "S" curve down her lower back and tight round hips. Her sexual escapades had earned her legendary status in high school.

I had a weekend job as a part-time janitor in that high school, a few years later, Jackie dropped by one morning for a visit. I was sweeping a classroom floor. She snuck up behind me as I pushed my broom and said, "Hey! How ya doin'?"

I spun around. "Sorry!" She said, "I didn't mean to startle you. I knew you were workin' so I thought I'd stop by an' give ya a break."

"Thanks!" I said. "I need a break." She stepped closer, put her arms around my neck and kissed my cheek; then slid her hands down my back, grabbed my ass and thrust her pelvis into my groin. "Hey, what's goin' on?" I asked.

"Whadda ya think?" She replied. Then she slid her hand around and rubbed my groin as she kissed my cheek. I stuck my hands under her tee shirt and caressed her small tight breasts. She undid my belt, unbuttoned and unzipped my pants, pulled her shorts down and bent over a desk. "This way!" she said. "I like it this way! Hard and fast!" We got into it and she moaned. "Harder! Faster! Harder! Faster!"

Darlene

Darlene was a young downer-head Hippie girl who shared an apartment with her brother, Fred, and two of his friends. She was about five-foot six with long, light brown hair, and bright blue eyes that glittered whenever she talked or smiled. She was a listener with a quiet sly sense of humor. When she and her boyfriend broke-up, Darlene decided to move to Oregon with Jackie and John.

We all arrived at Pat's in a caravan. Pat had prepared a great feast for the occasion. A huge selection of steaming bean and grain dishes were spread on the table; along with a variety of fresh organic vegetables, crisp green salads and a great pot of lentil soup. Fresh baked whole grain loaves of bread, still hot, lined the kitchen counter. Bottles of cold beer and wine were stacked and soaking in washtubs filled with ice on the front porch. We sat wherever we found a seat. I ate on the steps with John and Allen. The stereo blared back-to-the-land country blues that drifted into the front yard. Joints circulated, before, during and after the meal. We partied late then broke out our sleeping bags and crashed.

My wife, kids and Dee headed home the next morning, but I decided to leave on Sunday with Ken and Allen. We were having our coffee around the kitchen table and talking. Jackie was taking a bath. Darlene walked out of the bathroom and said, "Jackie wants a cigarette." I handed her one. "No, she wants you ta bring it to her."

"Why" I said.

"I don't know."

Jackie was stretched out in the tub when I walked in, smiling and squirming in the water. I lit a smoke, gave it to her then walked back to the kitchen to finish my coffee. After breakfast, Pat said, "Let's head ta Ann Arbor! You'll love it!" We agreed and stuffed into Allen's van, then drove into town for supplies, and to look around for a while. Ann Arbor was a college town with great record stores, bookstores and head shops. We shopped until mid-afternoon. Pat heard about a blues band that was playing in a local bar that night. We talked it over and decided to come back later and catch the show.

I was tired when we reached the schoolhouse, so I found a quiet corner in one of the rooms, covered myself with a sleeping bag and took a nap. When I awoke, Jackie and John were lying beside me. They were sleeping. I moved, Jackie stirred and John woke up. I closed my eyes and pretended to sleep. John stood up and left the room, then Jackie leaned over and kissed me, rolled on her side and wiggled her ass in my thigh. I spooned up. Our pants came down and I took her from behind. John threw back the curtain and stood over us, but we pretended to sleep. He couldn't see under the sleeping bags, but he could see how close we were. He stared at us for a minute in silence, then walked out. When we finished, I walked outside and joined John on the porch. We shared a joint and talked like nothing had happened.

Pat cooked another organic feast that evening, and then we cleaned up and headed back to town. John and Jackie stayed behind with their kids and two of the guys; the rest of us took off in Allen's van. There were no seats in the back of the van, so we all climbed in and sat on the floor. Darlene sat next to me. She was friendly, talkative and laughing. We shared a joint on the way. In the bar, we drank, danced and laughed while the band played and the crowd pushed us together. We pressed our lips to each other's ears to talk. We sat on the back floor of the van on the way back to the schoolhouse. I put my arm around her and she cuddled up. "Find a high bed to sleep on an' I'll join you later." I said.

She found one and I joined her. We floated on low flying clouds above the floor, blending with the cool summer-night air over Michigan. The next morning, when I climbed down from our cloud for a drink, Jackie was sleeping on the floor, beside the bed. After

40

breakfast, Darlene went west and I went east. I wrote her a letter later, but she never replied.

MAY DAY

Tin soldiers and Nixon's comin', we're finally on our own.
This summer I hear the drummin', four dead in Ohio.

Neal Young

May 4, 1970
Kent State University,
Kent, Ohio 44202

Dear Mom and Dad,

Today, the landlord tried to plant four roses in a concrete garden with a sledgehammer; but he only smashed the flowers flat and left them to dry in the sun. So, I picked them up and pressed their crushed petals between the pages of my books. Now, whenever I read, their clear blood forever drips from all these useless pages.

Love,

Your Wild-Eyed Sons and Daughters.

It was Monday. I should have been working. I didn't have any classes until late that afternoon. All of the news stories on the radio were about the student riots that had occurred at Kent State University over the weekend. A rally had been called at the university at high noon, and the National Guard had been called in to stop it.

I worked for a company that conducted property reappraisals for county governments in Ohio. My job was to reappraise houses in the little farm communities that surrounded my hometown. My boss permitted me to arrange my work schedule around my classes, so I commuted to Kent, three times a week, about forty-five minutes away.

I drove a dirty maze of highways through Akron, the tire and rubber capital of the country, and through the steaming sulfur air that suffocated the city. I could almost time my arrival to the minute. I appraised a few houses, snooping around and asking my required questions, but my mind was on the rally. I quit working about an hour later, stopped at a diner for a cup of coffee and a doughnut then headed to Kent.

The radio stations had ongoing reports of the riots that had occurred there over the weekend. It started on Friday, when President Nixon ordered the bombing of Cambodia. Students were outraged by this flagrant expansion of the Vietnam war. Groups of them gathered in small clusters around campus. Some made speeches while others listened. I saw the first pictures of the riots that night on the eleven o'clock news. The streets of Kent were shrouded in billowing clouds of tear gas. The usual end-of-the-week bar hopping ritual was out of control. Students broke windows and ran through the streets; chased by gas-masked, helmeted police; who caught them, clubbed them down with nightsticks, arrested them and dragged them to jail.

During the riots, members of the SDS, Students for a Democratic Society, a political activist group on campus, covered their arms and faces with Noxzema to counteract the burning effects of the gas. They wore leather gloves so they could pick up the hot canisters and throw them back at the cops. White-faced avengers traveled from rooftop to rooftop, avoiding the Pigs and moving quickly to hot spots where they were needed. On Saturday night, another student mob burned down the R.O.T.C. building, and fought off the firemen who came to put out the fire. On Sunday, Governor Rhodes declared martial law in the town and the National Guard was called in to establish order.

As I drove, I remembered my first class on campus. It was a history class held in a small lecture hall. I sat near a young man who was dressed in an army jacket, tie-dyed tee shirt, heavy boots and ragged bell-bottom jeans. He had a thin shaggy beard and long uncombed greasy hair hung over his eyes. During class, he slouched in his seat, arms folded. He seamed bored and uninvolved. He didn't ask any questions, say anything or take any notes. He hurried out after class and stood outside the door, distributing leaflets to the exiting students. The picture on the leaflet was a line drawing of a rising sun, with the letters SDS, Students for a Democratic Society, printed inside the sun. Rays radiated down to the earth and up to the sky. Under the picture was a Bob Dylan quote; "Twenty years o' schoolin' an' they put ya on the day shift." The leaflet announced a meeting that was to be held that night. I called home to let my family know that I was staying to attend.

The Young Socialist Alliance was another student activist group on campus. They had an information booth set up in the main hall of the history building. I hung out with them between classes. I got to know Joe; their short, curly-haired leader. Joe always wore old worn-out sport coats and ties whenever he represented the organization. His understanding of economic and political theory impressed me. The Alliance believed in nonviolent strategies to end war; but also believed in an evolutionary cultural overthrow of the rich, through grassroots organizing efforts of students and workers. Joe was a dedicated socialist, an infiltrator on campus working for a people's revolution.

He took the minimum number of courses necessary to be considered a student, so he could organize his end from the inside.

Students and workers didn't get along very well at that time though. The workers thought that the students were traitors who should love their country or leave it; and the students thought that the workers were red-neck bigots and war mongers. The idea that these groups could work together on anything seemed pretty unlikely to me; but I was drawn to the message and methods of the Alliance and helped them when I could. I manned tables and passed out leaflets, marched with them and attended rallies.

I reached the campus about eleven-thirty, parked my car and walked to the green. Soldiers in jeeps and on foot were moving through town. The football field had become a giant parking lot for their military trucks, tanks and other armored vehicles. I pressed through swarms of students and soldiers thinking about the pictures of helmeted police with Plexiglas shields I'd seen, beating and arresting protestors in Chicago. The crowd grew thick as I neared the rally. Lines of soldiers, eight to ten deep, formed a giant semicircle around the edge of the green. A crowd of civilian spectators gathered behind them. I squeezed through the crowd and saw two soldiers kneeling and fiddling with a jammed rifle. *If that gun's jammed,* I thought, *it's jammed with bullets. No, they're not real. They wouldn't shoot us; they're only blanks. They just wanna scare us away.*

I wormed through the crowd and crossed the green to the hill on the other side. Students gathered in small groups at the top; waiting for the rally to begin. Jars of Noxzema passed around, and students smeared it on their faces to counter the effects of the gas. Time passed and the crowd swelled. The sun was high. The sky was a perfect blue, eighty-degree May blanket over the day. Then, over a loudspeaker, a muffled male voice said, "This rally is illegal. You must disperse at once." We didn't; and that's when the tear gas came.

When the first canisters fell, billowing white smoke fractured the crowd. Students screamed and scattered, bumping into each other and falling down, trying to escape the burning smoke-filled air. Tears streamed down my face and blurred my vision. I tried to rub them away but that only made it worse. I stumbled through the crowd, searching for a breath of gas free air; then worked my way around the corner of a building on top of the hill to recover.

When the canisters stopped falling, a squad of twenty to thirty soldiers in gas masks moved across the green in military formation, then spread out and moved up the hill. When they reached the top, the student mob parted and allowed them to pass. The guardsmen marched through and stopped. The students closed in behind them. The guardsmen formed a semicircle and fired more gas into the mob, but the students picked up the canisters and threw them back. The guardsmen were swallowed in smoke. They formed up to move down the hill again, but the mob was so thick and unyielding that the guardsmen couldn't get through. I was closed in and couldn't move, or see what was happening.

The cracking of the M-16's ripped through me like an electric jolt. The crowd screamed and ran down the hill, breaking in a flesh-wave around me. I didn't know if the shots were aimed in my direction or not, but I ran. Gun thunder roared through my soul, pumping molten blood through my veins. The shots only lasted a few seconds but it seemed like forever. I broke free from the crowd, fearful of being trampled under the feet of the survival-seeking stampede, and reached

47

the safety of a cluster of small buildings at the bottom of the hill. A few students climbed a ladder to the flat rooftop of one of buildings and I followed. The shots had stopped but the crowd was still running. I saw two professors, talking and watching the action from the ground. A long-haired boy in a T-shirt and patched jeans ran up. He was waving his arms and screaming, "They been shot! They been shot!"

I climbed down from the roof and walked back up the hill. On my way, I passed the guardsmen as they marched back down and flowed into the olive green sea of their companions. When I reached the top, ambulances were screaming into the parking lot behind the building. I followed. Medics worked on wounded students, loading them into the ambulances and hauling them away. Red lights flashed and sirens raged. My friend, Max, ran up. He was wild-eyed as he gestured emphatically in the direction of the lot. "He's dead!" He said, "That one's dead!"

I looked to where he pointed and saw a body lying face down on the sun-bathed driveway. The body was clothed in a denim jacket and jeans. Long brown hair covered its face. It was lying cheek-flat on the pavement, slanting headfirst down a slight slope in the road. A rivulet of blood ran from under the head and glistened like a red ribbon in the sun. I looked away and wandered off to a spot behind some bushes. I sat there and watched the guardsmen, standing in formation like a khaki half-moon wall along the edge of the green. Students ran up and down the hill. Some stopped to scream at the soldiers from a safe distance then hurried on. Everyone moved like they had someplace important to go, but they were all going in different directions; a drastic contrast to the orderly discipline of the guardsmen. A news bulletin blared from a portable radio in the crowd. The newsman said that a shoot-out had occurred between students and guardsmen at the university. *A shoot-out?* I thought, *What are they talkin' about? We don't have any guns!*"

When the crowd broke up, I headed home in a numb dumb daze. That night, on the news, I saw a film clip of the shooting with a picture of the body I saw. His name was Geoffrey Miller. The clip showed a wiry-haired protester running up and wiping a red flag in Geoffrey's blood. Then he held the flag over his head in a clenched fist, screamed at the camera and ran on. Geoffrey made the national news the next day, when a photograph of his body appeared on the front page of every newspaper in the country. A young girl was kneeling beside him. Her arms were reaching up, and her pleading face was lifted to the sky.

The paper had pictures of the other students who were killed also. Two of them weren't even part of the rally. They were just changing classes in the wrong place at the wrong time. The only victim I knew was Allison Krause. We were in a Black History class together the quarter before. We were the only white students in the class, and took a lot of abuse from the young civil rights activists. I was always defensive and argumentative, while Allison was humble and graciously apologetic for the hateful crimes of our race. The article said that on the Sunday before the shooting, Allison had placed flowers in the barrels of the soldiers' guns as they stood at attention. "Flowers are better than bullets," she said.

SUMMERTIME

I am sitting of my front porch steps, smoking a joint on a warm mid-June afternoon. An old oak tree on the tree lawn shades the steps of the porch. Leaves rustle in a mild summer breeze. Neatly groomed homes line both sides of the brick-paved street. My family and I rent the house for a hundred dollars a month and pay the utilities. The front porch is about ten feet deep and runs the width of the house. Our neighbors are working or enjoying afternoon summer adventures. The street is empty and quiet. I stick my stereo speakers in the window; The Rolling Stones, Beggars Banquet, drifts into the street, "Waitin' for a factory girl." Electric blues blend with the sleepy neighborhood. I spot Frank walking up the street.

"I can smell that stinkin' thing all the way down ta the corner ya know." He says as he approaches.

"Yeah, but they don't know where it's comin' from." I reply. Frank sits down and I hand him a beer.

They don't know where it's comin' from? I think. *All ya gotta do is look at this place; Hippies comin' an' goin', all day an' night. The driveway is always filled with cars, and Joe and Weaser's psychedelic van is always parked on the tree lawn. The landlord threatened to throw us out a while back. "If you don't get rid of some of these folks," he said, "you'll have to leave. This house wasn't meant to accommodate all these people." Pat, Rick, Jerry, Denny, and their friends pop in from Toledo sometimes. Sue, Dee, Joe and Weaser are always here. Allen, drops by too, or Jackie and John. It's a day-glow freak-show of music, grass and organic food washed down with Boon's Farm Apple Wine or beer.*

51

Frank and I share the rest of joint and listen to the Stones. We talk for a while, then Frank gets up to leave. "John and I are playin' with Greg's band at a high school party outside o' town tonight. Ya wanna come along?" he asks.

"Sure!"

"I'll pick ya up about seven thirty or eight."

"I'll be ready." I reply. When Frank leaves, I head to the liquor store and pick up a pint of Bourbon for the night.

Frank and John pick me up around eight in Frank's van, an old bread truck converted into a camper. The van is square and clumsy. Doors slide open on both sides up front, and a sliding door opens in the back on the passenger's side; for curbside loading and unloading ease. The van has a comfortable driver's seat but the passenger has to stand a welded steel-plate well. Frank bolted a padded plywood seat to the floor there, so the person riding shotgun could sit eye-level to the dashboard. Exotic pictures and fabrics are pinned to the walls in back. Frank built a fold out platform bed there too, with a thin foam mattress, and installed an eight-track sound system with speakers placed in the four back corners. John Lee Hooker and Canned Heat boogie on tape as we ride. Frank and John sit up front. I sit in back on a beat-up trunk where Frank stores his clothes, sipping the bourbon and smoking another joint.

The party is a birthday celebration for a high school girl who just turned sixteen. A small stage is set up at one end of a large field beside her house. The girl's parent's hired Greg's band to play, and Greg asked Frank and John to sit in for a set. John plays guitar, flute, saxophone and piano, and approaches to his music like a mystic-poet.

When we reach the party, the place is crawling with

teenyboppers. Longhaired Hippie boys and girls talk, laugh and dance to rock rhythms blaring from hidden speakers; waiting for the band to begin. We stroll to the stage and I pass the bottle around to warm the guys up. Picnic tables are placed around the field. Frank, John and I find a table and sit. Kids mill and gather in small groups, sipping sodas and eating snacks. They drift from group to group, but each time a kid leaves a group, another kid arrives to take their place, so the groups stay about the same size, maintained by the constant motion of youthful energy seeking balance. Adolescent molecules bounce off each other in budding attempts at social interaction. Frank, John and I sip the bourbon and watch the teenage kaleidoscope turn, then Joey's sister, Angie, walks up with a couple of her friends. "Can I have a hit?" she asks.

She's a wild little blonde, cute and tough. I hand her the bottle. She takes a long slug and hands it back. I am sitting on the edge of the table with my feet dangling off the end, when one of Angie's friends walks up and stands next to me. She's elegantly thin with sculptured features softened by her young skin. Her bright brown eyes and hair glitter in the light. I rub her bell-bottomed calf with my sandaled foot. She presses closer. Then Angie says, "We gotta go!" and they leave.

Frank and John join the band for the second set. I walk to the stage with them and finish off the bottle with the band while they hook up. I'm ready to rock. They tune up, warm up and play. I wander around the field and listen to spirit songs, "It's Nature's Way" drifts through the night. I'm leaning against a tree, listening to the music, when that little teenybopper angel slides up beside me.

"Ya want some company?" she asks. "I'm Lori. This is my party. Ya wanna walk to the lake an' sit by the water?"

"Sure! Let's go."

Cricket chirps and birdcalls blend with the music and muffled breeze in the trees separating the field from the water. We sit on the grassy bank and talk. "Who are you anyway?" She asks. "Why haven't I seen you before?"

"My friends are playin' with the band and they invited me along. Is that okay?"

"Yeah, it's fine. I'm glad you came. I was bored. I didn't think it was gonna be any fun. It's a good party now. Why'd you rub my leg?"

"I was a little high an' loose I guess. I got carried away. I'm sorry."

"Don't worry about it. I liked it."

We talk and share a few laughs, then she asks, "Ya wanna go for a swim?

"Sure, let's go!" I say. We walk to the shore of the lake and undress. Her young nipples pop from her breasts, plump and pink. We wade into the water and swim around for a while then head back to shore. We lie down to dry in the warm night air and talk for a while, then I lean over and kiss her. She drives her tongue deep into my mouth. I climb on and press my groin to hers. She moans and rubs back, but will not permit me to enter. We kiss and caress a while then dress and head back to the party.

When John and Frank finish their set, we leave. Frank is driving and John is blowing his sax in the passenger's seat. I am sitting in back on the trunk where Frank keeps his clothes. I slid the side door open. A sudden summer storm blows up. Fat raindrops slant through the open door and splash against the side of the trunk, beating time with John's sweet sax.

"John! Play Summertime!" I say, and he breaks right into the tune; binding the night with the silk-blue ribbons unrolling from his holy horn.

FACTORIES

1.

A factory crouches in a cold gray dawn,

behind the scraped-down dusty facade of itself.

I hear rattling heartbeats of gray men.

Ghost-smoke rises like Gestapo jackal garlic mist

from drill-pressed holes of iron existence.

Steel history haunts the morning like a famished spirit

spectrum of the thread-worn promise of America.

2.

The Allison Tank Plant sprawls like an industrial whale beached on the Great Lake shore of Cleveland. The plant was built in World War II to manufacture military tanks and equipment for the government. There are three floors in the plant; one floor at ground level and two levels underground to protect it from attack. The floors are tiled with four-by-four cubes of wood placed side-by-side, cross grain face up and painted black. Plant smells fill the air, a mixture of stale exhaust fumes and metallic dust. Oil accumulates on the surfaces of all the old unused machines, stored along the aisles of the two underground levels like the skeletal remains of some ancient industrial civilization.

The plant was built in Cleveland because of the thriving steel and Great Lakes shipping industries that flourished there. It is a dim dusty place. The lights are just grimy tin shades covering bright bulbs attached to long cords dangling from the ceiling. They look like they have been hanging there since the war. The men look the same, dusty, abandoned, flesh-machines. The white men are pale and drawn. The black men look the same, but pale in a gray-brown way. High on the walls, great propaganda posters left over from the war encourage patriotic and careful behavior among the workers with slogans like, The Walls Have Ears or Loose Lips Sink Ships. The plant is so huge that all of the bigwig, upper level, white shirt and tie executives ride around in little electric Cushman cars all day, while the workers walk to their dreary I-beam stations.

The constant roar of the machines is so loud that the men rarely talk. It's so difficult to be heard over the noise. The foremen believe in an old school of management that is based on keeping the workers stirred up. They sneak around and watch the men while they work and say things like, "Get busy!" or, "What are you sittin' down for? Get to work, it ain't break time yet!" when they think the men are goofing off. The theory is, if the boss keeps the workers stirred up, they'll work harder to get even with him and teach him a lesson.

The only time any of the men smile is around two o' clock in the afternoon, when a secretary from the main office walks through the work area to deliver files to the foreman. She is tall and blond with long blond legs and tight hips. She wears high spiked heels and tight clothes that reveal every centerfold curve of her body. The men look forward to her visits. When she passes, they stop working and turn their heads to follow, smiling and dreaming amorous dreams of her jiggling Jell-O love.

3.

He held up his hand and said, "Look! Watta ya see?"
"I don't see anything." I said.

"I still have my fingers, don't I? If ya listen ta me, you'll keep yours too." Denny was the foreman of the little sawmill where I worked. He was a short, thin, bald man in a baseball cap who had no front teeth. His face was small but long, with only a few wrinkles. He clutched a smoking pipe in the tight-pinched lip-line of his mouth as he worked. He was a little suspicious of me at first. He looked down and glanced sideways as we talked. I was a new face in town, mid-west, back to the land immigrant to the backcountry; a flatland urban mountain man with long hair, beard and earring in a broad brimmed gray felt hat, worn flannel shirt, suspenders and patched jeans.

Denny was the foreman of the mill because he was the only one who knew how to set up and maintain the machines. He showed me how to set them up too; and whenever he adjusted or replaced the blades on the planer, ripper, or molder. He explained everything he was doing. He told me stories of men he'd known who'd lost various parts of their bodies to the blades. "Ya haffta pay attention." He said. "He just looked away for a second, an' when he looked back, it was gone."

A local canoe and snowshoe company owned the mill. We made ash stick frames for canoes, snowshoes and snowshoe furniture. My job was to turn pallets of ash boards into sticks; which were then steam bent into a variety of frames for the products. I worked with two Christians, Adam and Josh. Adam was a young, born again, Massachusetts immigrant. He and his family lived on a religious commune in town. Josh was a big, mentally impaired, religious fanatic son of an old local family. One afternoon as we were working, Josh stopped his machine, looked at me and said; "I saw the devil in your eyes and God told me to leave." He walked out the door and we never

59

saw him again. About a week later, Tim, a young drifter from New Orleans, passed through town looking for a job. He was a road-hard boy with thick sandy hair, great friendly grin and southern drawling street hustler's magnetic charm. Denny liked him and hired him on the spot.

Three women worked in the back room, lacing rawhide to the snowshoes and snowshoe furniture all day. Jill and Nancy were Connecticut girls who had just graduated from Green Mountain College and decided to stay in the area. Sheri was a middle-aged honky-tonk queen from Middletown Springs who always cracked raunchy jokes about her breasts, which bulged from her chest like honeydew melons. Men always stared at them when they talked to her. They would try to look away, but couldn't. Then she'd say, "Big, ain't they! You should see what I gotta do ta strap 'em up in the mornin'." Then she'd howl with laughter. Her breasts were so big that they got in her way while she worked. So, she sat sideways in her chair, lacing and cracking her raunchy jokes all day. When Denny thought I knew enough to run things in the mill on my own, he gave me instructions in the morning and spent his day in the back room, lacing with the women.

Easy time passed in our little factory, until the day some executive-assistant secretary from the main office ordered a truckload of lumber to be delivered when our forklift was in the garage for repairs. We couldn't send the load away; it would be too costly. So, we unloaded it by hand, board by board along a human chain, and re-stacked it on pallets on the ground. The job was huge. We worked a couple of hours and took a break. Denny wanted to reward our efforts; so he bought a case of beer at the little store across the street. We rested and drank, then continued to unload the truck, drinking as we worked. Another case appeared. People got giggly, dropping boards and staggering when they walked. Denny and the driver were pounding them down too. Sheri got red-faced and goofy. Her eyes were half-closed, bloodshot and glazed over. She was cracking one breast joke after another. We were all laughing, including the driver; who unfortunately didn't know one of our unspoken rules of appropriate shop conduct. The rule was that Sheri could make all the jokes she wanted to about her breasts, but the subject was off limits to everyone else. The driver said, "Betcha need two boyfriends fer dem tings."

Sheri went wild, swearing at the driver and jabbing her finger in his face. "He insulted my breasts!" she cried. "He can't do that! If any o' you guys are real men you'll do somethin' about it!"

Tim accepted the challenge and shoved the driver in the chest. His eyes were hard and steady, focused on the driver's face. "You owe her an apology!" he said.

"I didn't do nothin' an' I don't owe her nothin'!" The driver came back. Denny stepped between the two men, who were both at least a head taller than he was, and tried to cool things down. Tim reached over Denny to punch the driver, but Denny pushed Tim back. The driver said something I couldn't make out, then Tim pushed Denny aside and punched the driver in the face. The driver dropped his beer and covered his nose with both hands. Red pearls soaked his mustache and dripped to the ground as Sheri cheered Tim on.

"Hit 'im again!" she screamed, still wailing about how the guy had violated her. The driver dropped his hands and moved to retaliate, but I stepped in and stopped him. Denny was holding Tim back, who seemed satisfied with just punching the guy once. He listened to

61

Denny and calmed down. Then, Denny walked Tim into the mill and
the college girls took off with Sheri, who was still engaged in her
drunken weeping. I helped the driver with his nose. When the
bleeding stopped, he climbed into his truck and waited as Adam and I
finished unloading. We finished about one-thirty and the driver left.
Adam and I walked into the mill to make some sticks. Jill and Nancy
were talking to Sheri in the lacing room. Denny and Tim talked in the
corner of the shipping room, where the boxes were kept for our
products. Adam and I worked at the ripper and made a few sticks; but
it was a useless effort; so, I shut down early. "Adam, go home." I said.
"I'll punch ya out at quittin' time. There's nothin' ta do here."

　　　　"Thanks." he said; then he grabbed his gear and left. I walked
through the mill and found Jill and Nancy rolling Denny and Tim
around in two of the cardboard boxes we used to package our products.
They were laughing so hard that they didn't even notice me as I passed.
Sherri was gone. I walked outside and sat in the shade on a pallet;
smoking and relaxing in the leaf rustling summer silence until quitting
time. I passed Denny and Tim again on my way to the time clock.
They were sitting on the floor of the boxing room in a pile of crumpled
boxes. Denny was saying, "No! Don't get me wrong. I respect what
ya did but..." His voice faded as I passed, gathered my gear, punched
out, climbed into my truck and headed home.

DOWN AND OUT

1.

    I am an outreach soldier in President Johnson's War on
Poverty. My job is to make sure that needy families were cared for,
especially in emergency situations. It was late afternoon. It had been a
hectic day with all of the holiday food baskets I delivered to my clients
in the blizzard that started before lunch. Heavy snow fell all afternoon.
About four o'clock, I delivered my last food-basket to a family on the
third floor of an old Victorian house that had been converted into
apartments. I climbed a narrow, winding weather eaten staircase,
attached to the side of the house and covered with a three-inch layer of
snow, then knocked on the door. A young woman answered. She was
wearing a thread-worn cotton dress and grease-stained apron. She had
an infant perched on her hip. Her hair was snarled and pinned up with
bobby pins. "Hi," I said, "I'm from the Opportunity Council. I have
food for you."

    "Oh, thanks! It was late. I didn't know if you were coming."
She said, "You always do but I was a little worried. Would you carry
it in for me please?"

    "Sure! Where would you like it?"

    "On the table would be nice. I'll put it away."

    The kitchen was cluttered with toys. Dirty dishes and pots
were stacked in and around the sink. The baby on her hip was squirmy
and weepy. "Merry Christmas." I said as I left.

    "Thanks again!" she replied. I stepped through the door and
made my way down the stairs and back to the office. I wanted to leave
a little early, before the roads got too bad, but a call came in from the

Department of Welfare and I was the only one on duty. I met my clients at the Welfare office. Ed was in his late twenties. He, his wife and two kids were packed into a rust-eaten Oldsmobile. Everything they owned was stuffed into the trunk, strapped to the roof or packed into the back seat floor; where they had made a bed for their kids, on top of the suitcases and boxes.

Ed was short and thin with shaggy brown hair. His eyes were quick and alert, like a startled animal. His clothes were wrinkled and looked slept in. His hair and stubby beard were greasy, and he was missing a few teeth. Ellie, his wife, was younger than Ed. She was heavy-set with quiet cast-down eyes. Greasy strings of brown hair covered her face. Their kids, Bobby and Jill, were four and six. They wore grubby little coats that were too small and worn. Their eyes shined like stars in the skies of their dirty little faces. "May I help you?" I asked.

"We don't need no help mister." Ed said. "Like I told the other guy, I'm gettin' a job at Carroll's. I got laid off in Brattleboro an' they told me there was a Carroll's here. I got experience. They'll hire me."

"Have you talked to them? Do they need any help?" I asked.

"No, I was on my way to apply when I had a flat outside o' town. A cop stopped while I was fixin' it. He asked a few questions and kept the traffic away while I worked. When I finished, he led us here ta warm up. Tell me where Carroll's is an' I'll be on my way."

"I'll take you there." I said. "Your family can wait here." He agreed and we walked to my car. It was getting dark. The snow in the street was deep, almost to the bottom of the hubcap. I eased out and took off, sliding around the corner, and headed to Carroll's.

64

"I was gonna be the next night manager in Brattleboro, before they let me go." Ed said. "They didn't promise me anything, but I was there longest. I never missed any shifts an' took extra shifts as much as I could. If it wasn't fer the cutbacks, I'd be sittin' pretty."

"What if they don't need any help? Where're ya gonna stay? How long has it been since you've eaten?"

"I don't know." he said, "We had some burgers an' fries for lunch. When I get this job it'll all work out." Then he stared into the flurried darkness as we hurried on. I pulled into Carroll's and parked out front. Ed got out, thin coat flapping in the icy wind, and walked through the door. There were no Help Wanted signs in the windows, which were iced over and snow covered anyway. I couldn't see what was going on inside. I started the car to keep warm and waited. It didn't take long. Ed was out in about five minutes. He climbed into the passengers seat and stared out the window. His hard eyes were fixed on the night, jaw clenched and teeth grinding. He didn't say anything. I slipped into reverse, backed out and headed to the office. On the way, Ed snarled, "They didn't need nobody. I tried to tell the guy what happened; how long I worked in the other place an' what a good worker I was, but he wouldn't listen. He just walked away. I went after 'im but two other guys grabbed me an' made me leave. They owe me! I got time in! I got somthin' comin'!"

"We'll work it out when we get back to the office." I said. "For now, you need a place to stay for the night and something to eat. You might have to look for other work or temporary employment. In the meantime, I can get you services and emergency help. We'll work it out."

"They owe me." he said. Then he glared into the storm through the windshield until we reached the office.

Artie and the other guys had all chipped in for a bucket of chicken for the family. The mom and kids were gobbling down chicken legs, coleslaw and fries like it was Christmas dinner. Ed sat with them and ate. The guys in the office had chipped in for gifts for the kids too; a little truck for Bobby and a doll for Jill. Artie was a seasoned social worker that had managed to keep his job through a number of ever changing social programs of ever evolving administrations. He had seen many programs come and go over the years, as needy folks continued to file through his office. He was hard to deal with. He went by the book but helped me when he could. I followed him into his office while the family finished their meal.

"He didn't get the job." I said. "I can find 'em a place for a few nights an' emergency food; an' I'll get 'em signed up for services after the holidays. I'll set 'im up at the employment office after Christmas too."

"That's fine. It sounds good. If ya need any verification about anything, from anybody, tell 'em ta call me. I'll take care of it. Use my phone. Find these folks a place to stay for the night an' I'll get 'em there. Call your wife an' let her know you're comin'. Set these folks up an' I'll get 'em there. You go home!" I made a few calls and found temporary shelter for them, for a few nights. Artie and I walked out to give them the news. Ed and his wife were huddled and talking at the table when we walked over.

Ed looked up and said, "I think we're goin' on ta Burlington. I looked it up in the phone book. They gotta Carroll's there. If we leave now, we can make it before they close. They owe me! I got time in! Thanks, but we'll be on our way."

"No! Don't go!" I said. "The roads are a mess! You'll never make it! Wait 'til mornin' at least!" I was still talking when they stood up and walked out the door. Artie and I followed, pleading with them to stay; but they packed into their places. Ed started the engine and they drove off. The kids waved goodbye from the back window as they pulled away.

"That's the way it goes sometimes;" Artie said, " an' there's nothin' you can do about it. Forget it! Go home. Have a nice Christmas."

2.

I called home to let my wife to let know that I was on my way. "We'll wait 'til ya get here to eat." she said, "We'll let the kids open a present before they go to bed. It'll be fun. Be careful. See ya soon. Bye!"

I wished Artie and the guys in the office a merry Christmas and walked to my car. The storm was dying down and the streets had been reasonably plowed. I started the engine, eased into the road and headed home. The storm let up some on the way, but the road was snow covered and slippery. I turned on the radio. Sleigh bell Christmas songs jingled and jangled as I drove. My kids were waiting. I had their presents lying beside me on the seat. I found the Granny Doll Kim wanted, and the Enterprise Starship for Jason on sale at the mall, then picked up a necklace for my wife at the Farmer's Market Christmas Fair. It was a beautiful little piece, silver and jade, made by a little hippy girl in the country town of Shrewsbury. *Yeah! Tomorrow's another day.* I thought, *But what's it gonna be like for Bobby and Jill? Parked some empty lot maybe, cold and hungry with nowhere to go?* I wondered if we had enough wood for the night. I hate to be cold.

Just past Ira, ruts in the snow covered road forced the Ford into the jerky tracks of cars that had passed before. I slowed down. The wind blew snowdrifts across the road, filling the tracks and limiting my headlights' range. When I hit the first curve, just past Ira, the rear end of the Ford swerved to the left. I hit the brakes and swerved back to the right. The car slid from side to side. I turned the steering wheel back and forth, trying to catch up with the slide, but I couldn't. So I decided to let the car drift into the ditch that ran along the edge of the road. When I slid back though, the ditch disappeared and I soared over a six-foot ledge into the woods, then landed between two pines and crashed into a small birch.

My face smashed into the steering wheel, then I bounced back against the seat. I was thrown forward again but blocked my face with my arms. Everything was quiet except for the steamy clinking of the engine, still running in the dark. The headlights were broken so I couldn't see. Radiator steam poured from the crumpled hood. Blood gushed from my nose. It was broken too. I could tell by the way I could wiggle it around my face. The radio was still playing though. Bing Crosby was singing "White Christmas." I turned the car off, found a dirty rag on the floor and pressed it to my nose to stop the bleeding; then laid my spinning head back and closed my eyes.

When I came to; I felt achy, cold and broken. I shoved the driver's door open. A bitter wind hit me like a stiff branch slapping my face. I grabbed the bag of gifts and trudged away from the car, dizzy and freezing. I reached the ledge that I had soared over and climbed

68

the icy rocks on my belly, clutching the bag of gifts in my teeth. When I reached the top; I stood up, bundled up and started walking, hoping a car would pass. My body grew numb as I walked. Snow banks were piled along the edge of the road about three feet deep, so I walked in ruts of the road where earlier cars had passed. The night was quiet, except for the squeaky steps of my boots on the snow. I heard snowflakes falling on the tree branches through the ringing in my ears. My wife and kids were waiting. It was way past bedtime. I wondered if they'd still be up when I got home. My head ached. I couldn't feel my fingers. I shifted the bag of gifts from hand to hand and hiked on, hoping a car would pass and pick me up. I had about ten miles to go and thought about how easy it would be in a toasty car. I wondered if Ed and his family had made it to Burlington.

"One foot at a time. One foot at a time." I repeated to myself, stopping now and then to look back for a headlight. My kids' laughing faces drifted in the snow with the faces of Bobby and Jill waving goodbye from the rear window of Ed's car. I looked back once more, expecting the same black highway but a blurry set of headlights appeared a couple of miles back, headed in my direction. I stepped to the side of the road, stuck out my thumb and waited.

3.

A green Ford Pinto hurries through the night on the snow covered road between Rutland and Tinmouth. A man in his early twenties with dark brown slicked-backed hair and hard handsome face is driving. "Slow down Jake!" The passenger says. "What's the rush? Maggie'll understand! We'll get there. The road's a mess! Take it easy. We're not that late."

"I can't take it easy man! I told Maggie I'd be home at seven to help her get ready. She's gonna flip. We shouldn't o' stayed at the Saloon so long. It was my idea to have the party. I gotta get back ta help!"

"We'll get there, man! Relax! Maggie'll understand. She knows how close you and Ed are. She knows ya got good energy. It'll work out. Trust me. Slow down. Hey! There's a guy up there. See 'im?"

"Yeah."

"He's hitchiin' a ride. Let's pick 'im up. Nobody should be out in this."

"Okay. Whoa! Hold on man! We're swervin'!"

"Don't jam the brakes Jake, pump 'em, pump 'em!"

"I am pumpin' Mack!"

"Cut the wheel! Cut the wheel! You're gonna hit 'im! Look out!"

4.

Red, blue and yellow lights flash from police cars, emergency vehicles and tow trucks on a late night, snow covered country road. Emergency crews rush around and attend to an accident. A State Trooper and a young man talk at the edge of the road. The trooper is tall and lean, a seasoned veteran with piercing blue eyes. The young man is a little taller than the trooper, and he is wearing a worn gray parka and a stocking hat with earflaps untied and hanging down his bruised and smudged cheeks. His nose is bloody and he is clutching a bloody bag of gifts. "Good evening sir, I'm officer Willis," the

Trooper says, "I know it's late and you're hurt, but I have a few questions."

"That's okay. I don't mind, but could we sit in your car? I'm freezin'."

"Sure, no problem. It won't take long. When we finish, I'll take you home. Just tell me what happened."

"Well, there's not much ta say. I was on my way home after work and lost control of my car around Ira. The wheels got caught in ruts in the road and the rear end started slidin'. I tried to pull it out but ran off into a clump of trees a while back. I broke my nose, I think, but I'm alright. I wanted to get home so I started walkin'."

"I found your car about five miles back. I was looking for you; are you okay?"

"Yeah, I'm fine. I'm cold an' tired, but I'm all right. I just wanna get home."

"I need statement first, and if you seem okay to me, I'll take you home when we finish."

"Well, there's not much to say; after I crashed, I started walkin', hopin' for a ride. I saw their headlights comin' and stuck out my thumb. They tried to slow down when they saw me. I saw their brake lights come on but they were goin' too fast. They fishtailed like I did. They were headed right for me so I dove out of the way. They flew through the guardrail and over the ledge into that Maple. I climbed down to help them but the driver was dead. His chest was crushed by the steering wheel. The passenger was thrown through the windshield and was lying across the fender, bleeding. I tried to help 'im, but he died right before you got here. That's all I know officer. Can we go now? I wanna get home."

"Are you sure you don't want medical attention? You're pretty beat-up to me."

"No thanks. I'm okay. I made it this far. My wife'll take care o' me. Please, my kids are waitin'. I wouldn't mind a ride though."

"Well, you seem fit enough to me, I guess. Just sign this release an' I'll take ya' home." The drive is quiet. The Trooper's eyes are fixed on the road. The young man closes his eyes and dozes off until the cruiser pulls to a stop. "Here we are sir." The trooper says.

The young man wakes up. "Thanks for the ride officer, Merry Christmas." he says.

"No problem sir. Merry Christmas to you too." The Trooper watches and waits until the young man reaches the front door. A young woman greets him, hugs him and kisses him, then hurries him in, and out of the cold.

GROVE STREET

The Apartment

Patti and I lived in a little house in Belmont for three years. I first met her when we worked together at the food co-op. I was one of the directors of the co-op and she was a volunteer in the office. She had silky brown hair and big brown eyes. We talked and discovered that we had similar interests in art and literature. She was married to Adam, the marriage counselor who was trying to help my wife and I patch up our marriage. Patti and Adam had an open marriage, and had agreed that it was alright to date other men or women occasionally. My wife and I were experimenting with that idea also. So, Patti and I dated and fell in love.

She and Adam, and my wife and I divorced on the same day a couple of years later. A few months after that, Patti and I moved in together in a little house in Belmont, a little crossroads town about half an hour south of Rutland. We spent two carefree years there and then I lost my job. I was out of work for about four months, collecting unemployment. Patti came home from work one day and said, "I don't want to live with you any more. I'm not having any fun. You don't have any money! You don't contribute to or do anything! You don't even clean the house! I'd like you to leave. I'll be staying with friends for a few days to give you a chance to go. I spoke to the landlord about it, and he said that he would like you to leave also."

"Whatta ya mean? I can't leave! I don't have that much money, an' I don't have anywhere ta go!"

"You'll have to work that out." She said. I was outraged. I lunged at her and she backed up with a startled look on her face, like a

73

deer caught in headlights. I stopped myself and she ran out the door. The next day day, I packed as much as I could into the trunk and back seat of my car and moved out.

I stayed with some friends who let me sleep on their couch for a few days; then got a letter from the unemployment office along with my check. The letter said that my benefits had run out, and that no more checks would be coming. I had a small stash of cash that Patti didn't know about; so, with that money and the check, I got a haircut, bought three new shirts and two pairs of dress pants on sale, cleaned up and found a job as a furniture salesman.

Margie, a barmaid friend, told me about an apartment on Grove Street, next door to a TV repair shop about a block away from work. I checked it out. It was a clean little place with a kitchen, living room, bedroom and bath. I took it and worked out a deal with my boss at the store to buy a few pieces of furniture on credit; a small kitchen table, a couch, a desk and a small chest of drawers. I found three oak kitchen chairs and two oak parlor tables at a second hand place, and a swivel desk chair at a yard sale; then picked up my stereo and bed from Patti and my home was complete.

There were three other apartments in the house. The landlord's son and a few of his friends occupied one. The landlord owned the TV repair shop next door too. The picture window in my living room overlooked the parking lot in front of the shop and the street. Margie and her husband lived in the apartment house on the other side of the lot. The back entrance to my place was up a flight of stairs attached to the outside wall of the house. The stairs led to my second floor back door, which opened into the kitchen. I spent much of my time in the living room, sitting at my desk and staring through the picture window

74

that overlooked the street; watching cars and people pass. Bright sun poured soft light into the room through the window during the day. At night, a streetlight shined through, casting eerie edges of shadows' nocturnal angles of medieval gloom into the room.

Gypsy James

Gypsy James was a stranger in town. The bones of his long face were angular and sharp. He had long dark brown hair, a mustache and goatee. His eyes were quick bright strobe lights that darted around every room he entered. He wore heavy black engineer boots with silver buckles and a black beret; and bulky flower-printed shirts tucked into tight faded jeans held up by a thick, black leather belt with a silver buckle cocked off to the side. His outfits were always topped off with some ornately embroidered Arabic or Gypsy vest that had little jewels and mirrors sewn into the gold or silver design. He talked about poets like they were priests. He identified himself as a Neo-Bopster, Romanian Gypsy of Irish decent. He told me stories of Druids, White Witches and Celtic poets; and the sacred positions they held in ancient society. He believed in elves, fairies, goblins and trolls. When we walked in the woods and he talked, I could feel their presence. He told me stories of Celts, Wicca, Dada, Surrealism, Gypsies and white witches, Zen priests and Sufis, Pere Ubu, Siouxsie and the Banshees, Phil 'n the Blanks, *Dahlgren*, *The Broken Sword*, Beatniks, Genet, Rimbaud and Villon.

We dropped acid or ate magic mushrooms then snorted crystal meth or coke if we had it. After that, we'd smoke a little hash or grass, to take the edge off, and washed it all down with shots of bourbon and beer chasers. We ate speed beans and downers together, to get high in the middle, then we'd take a few pipe hits to see where that would go. When we were ready, we would hit the streets; drinking and visiting with friends in bars until closing time. I always blacked out on Quaaludes though, but somehow blundered through the nights; semi-conscious, but apparently friendly, polite and charming, or so I was told.

The Women

Sandy was a silkscreen artist who printed t-shirts for the food Co-op and Farmers' Market. She rented a corner space in Jeremy's studio. Jeremy was a conceptual artist from England who had turned to commercial art in order to pay the bills. His attic studio was the whole top floor of an office building on Center Street. Sandy had a slim tight body, short blond hair and long blond legs. I noticed her one day when I was visiting Jeremy. She was working on a tee shirt order while Jeremy and I talked. When she finished, she walked over to ask Jeremy about something. She was wearing one of her tee shirts, sandals and tight cut-off jeans. Her puffy nipples poked through her shirt, and her tight stomach and lower back curved down and around her firm hips, then along her long athletic thighs. I met her in the Café a few nights later. We talked and drank for a couple of hours. When last call came and the Café closed, we went for a midnight swim at the gorge and made moonlight love on the bank of the Cold River.

Marcy was a friend of Patti's. She was short, with dark brown hair that hung to her shoulders. She had damp brown eyes, and lips that parted slightly whenever she smiled. I was drinking a beer at the bar in the Café one night when she walked in. It was late and the place

76

was almost empty. She sat on the stool next to me. We talked and laughed, and she bought me a couple of drinks. When last call came, she smiled and touched my hand. "What?" I said.

"Whatta ya think? We're consenting adults, aren't we? The only question left is your place or mine?"

"My place is closer." I said.

"That's fine." She replied, so we left.

When we reached my apartment; we climbed the back stairs and entered, then sat on the couch and talked. I scooted closer to her, put my arm around her, pulled her close and kissed her. She kissed me back. "Oh!" she said, "I had no idea."

We kissed, hugged and rubbed around for a little longer, and then I said, "Ya know, we'd be more comfortable in the bed." She agreed, so we walked into the bedroom, undressed and crawled under the covers. I kissed her neck, then on down her tight torso; then caressed, licked and kissed her budding breasts and offered myself on the altar of her body.

Jan was another friend of Patty's who picked me up in Murphy's on another night. She was as tall, as tall I was. The lines of her face were hard, angular and sharp. She had coarse, curly black hair that she wore in an Afro. A big white streak ran through the left hemisphere of her head like captain Ahab or the bride of Frankenstein. She was sitting alone on a stool at Murphy's when I walked in. "Join me!" she said, "I'll buy ya a drink."

I sat next to her, and we drank and talked for a while, then she rubbed my leg and said. "I have to go now. Would you like to come along?"

"My place is closer." I said.

"Let's go!" she replied.

Sara was a young hippy girl who painted pictures of people with no faces. She had angel blond hair and deep blue eyes. Her breasts were full and firm. I admired them once when we bathed together in the Cold River.

She crashed at my place late one night, after a bar hopping ceremony. She was between apartments and sleeping around with friends. She undressed and crawled into bed beside me. I got stiff, snuggled up and rubbed against her. "Hey!" she said, "What's goin' on?"

"Whatta ya think? If you're not into it, it's okay."

"No, it's alright, I been thinkin' 'bout it too. I'm dirty though. I wanna shower an' clean up first."

"Go ahead." I said. "I'll wait."

Rita was Sara's a friend from New Jersey. She visited one weekend. I ran into them in the Café that night and bought a round of drinks. Rita drank Scotch, straight up. She was tall and thin with creamy skin and round brown eyes. Her curly blond hair hung in feathery ringlets that brushed her pale cheeks and sleek neck. The night passed, and Rita and I flirted and talked. Then, Sara said, "Come on Rita! we gotta go."

I kissed Rita's ivory neck before she left, then drank until the bar closed. I started home but didn't want to be alone; so I headed to Sara's, hoping that Rita was still awake. I knocked on the door and Sara answered. "Come on in!" she said. Flash, Sara's boyfriend, was there too. Rita was a third wheel, unwelcome and in the way. She was lying in a sleeping bag on the floor when I walked in. I took a chance, laid down beside her and she pressed close.

"Ya know, we'd be more comfortable at my place." I said.

"Okay, let's go!" she replied, so we left. When we reached my apartment, I led her up the stairs, through the door and directly to the bedroom; then undressed and slid into bed. Rita peeled off her top and crawled across the bed on her hands and knees; then kissed me and pressed her breasts in my face. I hugged her and turned her on her back, then kissed on down her sleek neck and licked her slim torso; then unzipped her cut-offs, pulled them off, climbed on and slid in. The next morning, when I woke up; I showered, shaved and headed to work. Rita was still sleeping when I left.

Karen was an interior decorator at the furniture store. She designed contract furniture packages for out-of-state customers who had purchased second or third homes in ski areas. She was about five-foot five or six, but looked taller; due to the elegant length of her fingers, arms and legs. Her young face was framed in wavy brown hair that hung to her shoulders. A light scattering of freckles ran across her nose and cheeks. Her hips were firm and round. All she had to do was lean back a little bit to sit on the edge of her stool. She always looked good, whether in work jeans and a flannel shirt, or in a slinky little dress. She wore a shoulder-less, flower-printed sundress to work one day, held up in front by thin straps tied in a bow at the back of her neck. Whenever she bent over, I could see her puffy nipples nesting there like two plump little pink birds. The biggest problem with Karen was her six-foot-four, Greek-god boyfriend; so, I knew that the best I could ever hope for was, maybe, second place. Second was okay with me though, so I flirted with Karen anyway.

The store held an inventory reduction sale in a huge warehouse on the edge of town one Saturday. The was well advertised and mobbed with customers. We sold the place to the walls. After the sale, I asked Karen out for a drink to celebrate and she accepted. We walked to Murphy's and talked along the way, then sat on bar stools, ordered our drinks and talked as we sipped them. She was wearing tight jeans and a loose fitting blue flannel shirt tucked in at the waist. The top button of her shirt was unbuttoned. I saw her plump pink nipples popping from her breasts as she leaned on the bar. When we finished our drinks, she walked me home.

When we reached my apartment I asked, "Wanna come in for nightcap?"

"No thanks," she said, "Not tonight anyway, some other time maybe. I have to get home."

"Anytime's fine." I said. Then I slipped my arms around her waist and hugged her. She reached around my neck and squeezed. I pulled her close and kissed her cheek. She slid her hand down my back and rubbed my ass; then slid it around and stroked my groin.

"Please, come in!" I pleaded.

"I want to! I really do! I just can't." she said. I pulled her close and kissed her. She kissed back. I kissed her neck as I unbuttoned her shirt and bent her back over the fender, and then kissed her puffy nipples for a while before she left.

I met Barb in the Café on another night. She was sitting on a barstool when I walked in. She looked at me and smiled. I sat on the stool next to her. She had long dark hair and sleepy brown eyes. Her face was pale and hard, but pretty. Her mouth was her most charming feature; it got a little crooked when she smiled or talked. She was a nurse at the hospital and was married to a lawyer, but was in the process of a divorce. We talked a while and she invited me to her apartment for coffee when the bar closed. I accepted, so we walked to her place, had our coffee and I stayed the night. She liked to be on top, breasts bouncing in time with her grinding and pounding as she moaned.

I met Diane in the Café too; she had light blue eyes, creamy skin and dark brown hair that hung to her shoulders. I was a little drunk and obsessed by her beauty, so I walked over and said, "I think I love you." She gave me a dirty look, stood up and stormed away.

I saw her in the Café, a few nights later, and our eyes hooked up again. She walked to my table and took a seat. "Why'd you say that the other night?" she asked. "It was so stupid!"

"Yeah, I know. I was a little lonely, an' high an' I guess, and you looked lonely to; so I took a chance. Sorry."

"It's okay. I been thinkin' about it. I liked it." She said. So we drank and talked. She was a nurse. She and her lawyer husband had moved up from Boston two years earlier, but were in the process of a divorce. When the bar closed, she said, "Well! Whatta ya think? We're consenting adults, aren't we? The only question left is your place or mine?"

"My place is closer. I'm just two blocks away." I said.

Tammy was a seamstress in the drapery department of the furniture store. She was about forty years old, but she had a body of a much younger woman; shapely little breasts and hips, blond hair, soft lips and pale blue eyes. Her hair was a blond frame around her pale pretty face. She was married but she and her husband had separated. The rumor around the store was that she was seeing the foreman of the warehouse on the side.

We worked late together one Saturday night. We talked and flirted, then she offered me a ride home when the store closed. "I just live down the street." I said. "I can walk."

"Come on, I'll give you a ride anyway. Oh," she said, when we pulled into the lot, "so this is where you live."

"Would you like to come in and see the place?"

"No thanks, I have to get home. Some other time maybe, when I'm not so rushed."

She dropped by a few nights later. I was sitting at my desk and looking out the window when she pulled into the lot. She parked her car, climbed my stairs and knocked on the door. I answered. "Hi!" I said, "Come on in." She was wearing a black leotard top and a blue flower-print wrap-around skirt. Her hard little nipples poked through the fabric.

"I was just passin' by an' thought I'd stop in for a visit. Is that okay?" she said."

Sure! Come on in," I replied. We sat on the couch and talked. She moved closer to me. I put my arm around her, laid her back and kissed her neck; then she hugged me and pulled me close.

"Oh, I had no idea!" She said. She stopped by a few other times after that, until she and her husband split up. Then I developed a habit of dropping by her place when the bars had closed and I hadn't scored.

When her ex-husband found out what was going on, he sent a message to me through one of his friends. The guy approached me in the bar one night and said, "Listen up! Tammy's husband sent me tell you that if you don't stop seeing Tammy, you'll meet a couple of his friends from New Jersey who will convince you that what you are doing is wrong."

I told Tammy about it the next day, and she said, "Yeah, it's probably true. I saw him beat two guys out cold once in a bar. They pulled knives on us. He beat 'em and took their knives away, then kicked them a few more times while they were down. They weren't moving when we left."

I was sitting at my desk, staring at the street one night, when Margie came home. She unlocked her door and stepped through. Her living room light came on, then her bathroom light. Her bathroom window was a small opaque square located above her tub. I saw the silhouette of her head bobbing around as she showered. *This might be a good time for a visit,* I thought. Then I thought, *No, too obvious. I'll wait 'til she's done.*

Her head disappeared from the window and a light came on in her bedroom. Her bedroom window was tall and wide. The shade was up and the curtains were pulled back. She walked past the window, naked. I sat up and leaned forward for a better look. Her breasts were full firm cones and her slim waist curved down her round hips and flat stomach, then on down her tight thighs. I tried to fill my eyes before she pulled the shade, but she didn't pull it down; she left it open and stood in front of her mirror, brushing her long dark hair. *This might be a good time for a visit.* I thought. I put on my jacket, stepped out the door and hurried down the stairs. The landlord's son and his roommates were standing in the picture window of their apartment as I passed. They were watching Margie too, smoking cigarettes and drinking while they took in the show. They didn't even notice me as I passed. I moved across the lot, through her front door, up the stairs to her apartment and knocked. She was wearing a burgundy bathrobe when she answered. The top curves of her breasts bulged from the "V" of her chest where the robe came together.

"Hi," I said, "I was just passin' by on my way home, and an' thought I'd drop in for a visit. How ya doin'?"

"I'm okay." She smiled. "Come on in." We sat on her couch and talked. She moved closer. I put my arm around her and rubbed her back. I kissed her and she kissed back. She squeezed me as I caressed her breasts. "Listen," she said, "we can fool around for a little bit, but I can't sleep with you. Is that okay?"

"Yeah. That's fine." I replied. So I loosened her robe and kissed her neck as I massaged her breasts, then slid my hand on down her torso and stroked her slippery womanhood. She moaned and pressed her pelvis hard against my hand and squirmed, but refused to go any further, so I left. My neighbors were still standing on their porch, watching her window and hoping for more when I passed. I waved to them but they didn't wave back. I sat at my desk and stared out my window again. Margie had returned to her mirror, naked and brushing her hair once more. When she finished, she wiggled into a loose fitting tee shirt, then crawled into bed and turned out the light.

A week or so later, when Margie's boy friend was out of town on a business trip, and I thought Margie might need some company, I stopped by for another visit. She answered the door in a clingy purple sweat suit. "Come on in." she said. Then we sat on her couch and talked. I moved closer to her and she didn't move away, so I put my arm around her and her kissed my cheek, then ran my free hand up under her shirt and kneaded her breasts. She squirmed a little and pulled me close. So I worked my hand down her stomach until I reached the waistband of her sweat pants; then untied the strings and slipped my hand down to the coarse vortex of her sex. A sticky river ran through her magic valley. She pressed hard against my hand and moaned.

Then, a knock at the door interrupted us. Margie jumped up to answer it. "Is Jeff here?" I heard Jim say. He had never been to my place, but knew that I lived on the second floor of a house next to a TV repair shop. So, when he walked by and saw the lights on at Margie's apartment, he thought; *this must be the place!* "Sorry ta bother ya man," he said when he walked in, "but me and Karen just had a big fight! We're gonna split up! I gotta talk ta ya!"

Karen was Jim's on-again, off-again X-wife. They had been on the road together for many years and were connected by a love-hate dependency from which neither could escape. I left with Jim and we headed to the Café, had a few beers and talked for a couple of hours, then he left and I walked home. Margie's apartment was dark when I got back. I climbed the stairs and found a note pinned to the door. The note said, "I'm sorry. I made a mistake. I love my boyfriend. I was lonely and took advantage of you. I apologize for leading you on like that. It'll never happen again."

Sorry! I thought. *I'm the one who's sorry!* Then I thought *if Charlie's foolin' around, Sharon might be lookin' for company.*

Sharon was tall and slim with shoulder length light brown hair, big brown eyes and a thin sly smile that never quite revealed her thoughts or feelings. Whether she was standing, head high and classic in a room or floating into it like a dancer, every space she occupied surrendered to her presence. I ran into her in the Café one night. We found a quiet table in a corner, had a couple of drinks and talked until the bar closed. After that, she stopped by the furniture store a few times while I was working. She brought little gifts for me; a smooth black stone she found on some island, and a brown velvet bow tie she thought would look good on me. She snuck into my place one night while I was sleeping. She shook me gently and kissed me. I woke up and kissed her back. She undressed and climbed into bed. Her body was long and hard; tan skin, dark eyes and clean angular features like Egyptian art.

She stopped by a few nights later; but I had been out drinking with Sandy, who had decided to spend the night. It was about two in the morning when Sharon snuck in. The room was dark and she couldn't see Sandy lying beside me, so she walked in and sat on the edge of the bed, then shook me, but I didn't wake up. Sandy woke up but pretended to sleep. Sharon whispered in my ear and shook me gently, so Sandy moved to let her know she was there. When Sharon saw the movement, she stood up and hurried out. In the morning, I woke up, showered, dressed and went to work. Sandy was still sleeping when I left.

I ran into Sharon on the street, on my way to Café' that night. "How ya doin?" I said.

"I'm good. I stopped by for a visit last night." she replied. "I wanted to surprise you but you had company, so I left." I fumbled and stumbled over and around possible words and explanations flashing through my head, but found nothing meaningful to say. She walked away and I headed to the Café. Jim and Sandy were sitting at a table in the corner when I walked in. I ordered a draft and joined them. They smiled when I sat down. Jim shook his head and said, "Man, you're too much."

Sandy said, "You better get a flag for your mailbox to let all your girlfriends know when your bed is occupied."

Mary was Sandy's high school friend of from New Jersey who visited one weekend. She had curly blond hair and a smooth creamy complexion that she concealed with layers of makeup. Her legs were long, hard and muscular; but looked round and soft. She was addicted to running, a Bruce Springsteen fan, Born to Run on the cusp of Libra and Scorpio. She had a tough New Jersey attitude which, when coupled with her curling venomous stinger-tongue, made her a lethal weapon. I called her The Jersey Resistance. If we were in a bar and a guy hit on her, she wouldn't just turn him down; she'd verbally attack him and cut him off, leaving him emotionally wounded and bleeding on his stool. She did it so skillfully, and with such razor contempt, that the only thing her victims could do, was to shrink off to a dark corner and hide in their drinks when she finished.

I was having a beer in the Cafe' one night, waiting for the music to start, when Mary, Sandy and Sandy's young nephew walked in. We found a table on the deck outside, sat together and talked. When the music started, Sandy, left to get her nephew home to bed but Mary stayed. The music was good and Mary was friendly. One of her front teeth was a little crooked. When she smiled, her lips twisted into a funny little shape that perfectly fit her pretty face. The night passed and we drank and talked until the bar closed; then she walked me home and stayed the night. She was married but was in the process of a divorce. She invited me to visit her in New Jersey. "You mean, stay at your place?" I asked.

"Sure!" She said.

"What about your husband?"

"He won't care, and I don't care if he does. I have my room and he has his. Come on down, we'll go into the city an' play. We'll have a great time." So, I caught the train to Grand Central Station a couple of weeks later. Mary picked me up. She was wearing a slinky yellow dress and looked like a spring flower sprouting from the station's greasy floor; littered with trash, newspapers, and musicians playing for tips, and down and out homeless folks begging for spare change. The driver's window was open on the way to Mary's house. The wind blew her dress back, revealing her hard thighs and lacey treasure. Her husband had his room and Mary had hers. I slept with Mary.

The Ghosts

October arrived and the days grew short and night fell early. I got home from work about seven o'clock. The street was dark and cold. Brown leaves twisted, broke loose and drifted from the tall gray maples and oaks that lined the street, and then scattered over the pavement in a quick wind. I raised my collar. The two great maples in front of my house were jerking wildly as I approached. Leaves and papers danced with the wind in streetlight shadows. I started across the lot then saw a shadow dart between the repair shop and the house, and meld into the shadows of the buildings. A piercing scream came from a corner of the shop. I ran to the bottom of my stairs and started up. I looked back and caught a glimpse of the shadow as it slipped behind my building. I bolted upstairs, stumbling and fumbling with my keys on the landing, unlocked the door, burst through and slammed it behind me.

I sat at my desk, drank a beer and smoked part of a joint to calm down. A tree branch banged against the window. The spotlight of the parking lot created ghostly shadows of branches that danced around the lot, through the window and into my room. A dark figure in a long coat and broad brimmed hat ran under the window, screaming. It reached the end of the building and rounded the corner. The screams grew fainter; then louder again as the figure passed once more beneath my window. The screaming stopped then and the shadow disappeared. I leaned back in my chair.

The front door of the apartment building opened and slammed. Heavy feet pounded up the stairs. "BOOM, BOOM, BOOM," then "BANG, BANG, BANG," on my door. I jumped up. The heavy feet stomped down the stairs and slammed out the front door again. I sat still and waited. Shadows jerked around the room. The front door opened and slammed once more. Then, "BOOM, BOOM, BOOM," up the stairs, "BANG, BANG, BANG," on my door, and "BOOM, BOOM, BOOM," down the stairs and "SLAM."

I put my coat on and headed out the door and down the stairs to the sidewalk, then hurried on to Center Street. As I walked, I looked back occasionally to see if the shadow had followed. The closer I got to the bar though, the better I felt. I wanted to find Jim. He knew about these things. He had a visionary understanding of their meanings. I hit Murphy's but Jim wasn't there. The place was packed with strangers. I decided to have a beer and wait, to see if Jim would drop by. I found an empty stool next to a guy I didn't know. "Excuse me," I said, "is anyone sittin' here?"

He glanced sideways at me and snarled, "I guess you are now." I hesitated, but it was the only stool open at the bar and I wanted to sit. *I'll have a beer an' wait. When Jim comes in, we'll leave.* I thought. I sipped my glass and checked the guy out from the corner of my eye. He was short and stocky. He was wearing a worn wool knit hat; greasy uncombed hair fell to his shoulders, which were hunched over and hard as he leaned on the bar. He stared straight ahead. His eyelids drooped halfway over his blood-shot eyes. He hadn't shaved for a couple of days. He looked at me, nodded his head at the bartender and said, "Ya know, in a couple 'o minutes I'm gonna order another beer an' he's gonna shut me off an' I'm gonna haffta shoot 'im." Then he returned to his drink.

I sipped my beer and didn't say anything. He looked at me again and said, "I gotta forty-five right here," as he patted his left side. He was wearing a bulky, threadbare, grease stained zip-up sweatshirt; so I couldn't tell if he had a gun or not.

"Why do you have to shoot 'im?" I replied.

"'Cause I'm just in the mood," he said, "an' if I want another beer, he better get me one."

I couldn't tell if he had a gun or not, but he had enough attitude to kill everyone in the place if he did, and I didn't want to be around when the shooting started. I walked into the kitchen. Will, the owner of the place and head cook, was sitting at a table talking with the kitchen staff when I walked in.

"Listen Will!" I said, "I'm sittin' next to a guy out here who says he's gonna shoot Bill if he shuts 'im off."

"Do you know him?" Will asked.

"No! Never seen 'im."

He walked to the door and yelled, "Bill, come here!" Bill walked in and Will asked, "Do you know the guy sittin' next to Jeff?"

"Nope, never seen 'im before."

"Shut 'im off." Will said.

What's he doin'? I thought. *What if the guy starts blastin'?* I left the kitchen, squeezed through the crowd to the door then hustled down to the Cafe. I wanted to be out of there and off the street before the shooting started. Jim was sitting at the bar when I walked in. I sat next to him and told him about the dark spirit at my apartment and the guy at Murphy's with the gun, and he said, "Ya got messengers man. Ya better pay attention."

Jim left a little later, but I stayed until the bar closed. The music was lousy and I didn't meet anyone, but I didn't want to go home. When I finished my last-call draft though, I had to leave. I walked slowly to my place, hurried across the lot, up the stairs and through the door, then undressed, crawled into bed and fell asleep. A little while later, I woke up to loud voices coming from the street. I got up and looked out the window. Two teenage boys were yelling at a third boy who was bigger than they were. The big boy's speech was

91

slurred and his gestures were jerky. One of the shorter boys was screaming, "You son-of- a-bitch, you knocked my tooth out! Why'd you do that? I don't even know you! I didn't do anything!" The bigger boy was trying to apologize but his slurred words fell on deaf ears.

I went back to bed but awoke to screams coming from the landlord's son's apartment about an hour or so later. I got up, walked into the kitchen and looked out the window. Four police cars and an ambulance were in the parking lot. Blue and red lights flashed; emergency workers and cops were running around. One cop stopped, looked up and saw me in the window. He pointed his flashlight in my direction and put his hand on his gun. He called to the others, "Up here!"

Two more cops ran up with flashlights pointed at me. I showed them my raised hands and opened the window. "Who are you?" one asked, "What are you doing?"

"I live here." I said. They studied me for a minute then moved on. Cops and emergency personnel headed up the other set of stairs and brought a guy down on a stretcher; then stuffed him into an ambulance and drove off with lights and sirens blaring.

The next day, the paper ran a story about it. It turned out that the guy the cops took away was a friend of one of the guys who lived in the other apartment. The shooter had stopped by for a visit, got drunk and depressed about losing his job or girlfriend or something, then went to his car to get his rifle so he could shoot himself at their place. He sat in a chair for couple of hours with the barrel tucked under his chin as the other guys tried to talk him out of it. In the end, he only shot himself in the leg and the emergency crew was called in to rush him to the hospital. I also found out that the dark spirit I saw was just the landlord's mentally disabled son who was just trying to say hello.

SALOON AFTERNOONS

The Mountain Amazon

I stopped at the Saloon after work for a beer. I was leaning on the bar, talking to Chris and Nancy, when an attractive young woman walked up. She was young enough to be my daughter but big enough to look me in the eye. She got in my face with a cold steel stare and snarled. "You're always surrounded by women, aren't you?"

"I don't know, never thought about it." I said.

"Well, I thought about it and I think you're an asshole." She replied; then turned and walked away. Chris and Nancy backed off then and left me standing alone, stunned and curious. I looked around. The girl was drinking with some friends at the other end of the bar. She was a blue-eyed, blond-streaked, brown-haired, pony-tailed down country skier in a blue nylon ski suit, Connecticut or Massachusetts maybe. She was tall and hard, a She-Warrior as big as I was.

She looked back and walked over, "I still think you're an asshole," she said. "but your hat and earring turn me on. I noticed you when you first walked in. You wanna come back to the mountain with us and play?" as she gestured down the bar to her companions; a row of young coeds laughing, talking and sipping drinks with soft lips in the smoky blue light. "You can fuck 'em all if you want to." She said. "I won't fuck ya though, I'd break ya in half."

I looked at her and thought; *She's right. She'd grab me by both cheeks of my ass and use me like a human dildo.* "Thanks, but no thanks," I responded, "I'm broke already."

The Bad Blood Blues

Sweet, down-home country blues play, Sonny Terry and Brownie Magee on tape, and Brownie says, "You got bad blood baby, I think you need a shot." An' I think, *He's right, a shot o' Bourbon maybe, or a few new cloud word arrows piercing my bulls-eye language with the hot blue bullet holes of my voice.*

Yesterday, drunk and driving back from Doug's, I stopped to piss at the side of the road. The bank was steep and the ground was glazed over in freezing rain. I unzipped and whipped it out; then slipped down the icy slope, exposed and vulnerable. I reached out to grab something to stop my fall, and gouged three jagged rips in the side of my left hand on barbed wire that was frozen, spikes-up, in the cold hard mud. I got to my feet and climbed the slippery bank to the truck, dripping blood in the dirty snow. I searched through the junkyard bed of my pick-up truck for a bandage and found a greasy wool seat cover. I wrapped my hand in it and nursed my wound as I drove on to the Saloon.

The Messenger

It is early August. I stop at the Saloon after work for a Pounder. A Pounder is a sixteen-ounce glass of Genny Cream Ale on draft for a buck. Usually, I drink three or four, or nine or ten, then call home to tell my wife that I'll be there in about an hour. She knows this story though, and she also knows that I never make it. I've been doing this for months. She's bound to get sick of it soon. The Saloon is packed, wall-to-wall. I find a spot near a group of friends. We are drinking, talking and having a good time when I notice a hard looking guy staring at me from across the room. He is a stranger. He is smiling a mocking, scornful smile, and jabbing his finger in my direction. He says something to the guy next to him then motions to me with a waving arm, signaling me to join them like he wants to tell me something. I have never seen him before, so I motion for him to come to me, preferring the safety and support of my companions. As he walks over I think, *who does he think he is anyway, mocking me in my hometown bar?*

I drunkenly prepare for battle. I am on a barstool. He is standing. I decide to smash him in the face with my Pounder glass if there's any trouble. He walks through the protective shield of my friends, breaks the fragile planes of my space and stands right next to me. He is short and stocky with long greasy brown hair and a rough beard, mid-thirties maybe. He has the strong dark arms of a laborer. His eyelids droop halfway over his vision. He drapes a heavy arm around my shoulder, leans into my face with a wide stubby grin and says. "Just what do you want anyway?"

His words hit me like an iron fist. I go limp and numb. *What do I want?* I think. *It's a fair question for which I have no answer. How did he know to ask it? Who is he? Where is he from? What does he want? Is he a messenger of some kind?* I feel like I've met him before. He has come to me in many disguises. This time, a blue-collar bar-fighter. "I don't want anything," I lie, "I'm fine." He nods and smiles, then turns and shuffles away.

That Low-Down D.U.I.

I was headed home after work and stopped for a few beers at The Saloon. A few too many according to the deputy sheriff who stopped me on my way home; D.U.I. at .15 on the liquor scale, ticket and court date. I was going to New York in the morning to fix some fat-cat's swimming pool for cash, but the weatherman is predicting rain. So, here I sit alone and tipping these blues in a bottle back again; and the deputy sheriff, an' Sonny and Brownie say, "You got bad blood baby. I think you need a shot."

And I say, "If it wasn't for bad blood boys, I wouldn't have no blood at all."

INSIGHTS OF ALTERED STATES

I keep a bottle of Vodka in the back of my file-cabinet drawer and hit on it in the morning with a couple of beer chasers. Then I smoke a bowl of dope and drink a couple of cups of coffee to even it out.

Soul bearing requires a warrior's courage. Enter every battle expecting to die. Is there nothing in your life worth losing everything for? All stars are possible beyond the borders of reason. Sometimes though, it gets hard to see through foggy misunderstanding or to formulate any starry essence of reason.

I am wearing my Salvador Dali baseball cap tonight. I want to play a game of surrealistic softball; when lobbed pitches turn into slow diving doves in light descent, and bats flap like wooden wings whiffing the air. Invisible balls drop in fielders' gloves, reaching like great leather hands stroking swirling clouds airbrushed on a velvet sky.

I woke up at 3:00 AM, startled by a dream. In the dream I had taken my guns to school, a 9 mm and .357 Magnum Smith and Wesson. I found them in my bag at lunchtime. *What if some kid took them and shot up the place, or sucked on a bullet himself?* I thought. I couldn't stand the idea of it, so I went home and searched for them under the dresser. They were gone. In their place I found a little case filled with tiny toy soldiers. I jumped out of bed, and checked for the guns, to make sure they were there. When they checked out, I drank a beer and smoked a cigarette while I thought about the horror that drove me to stop drinking the last time; and wondered what madness it would take to drive me there again.

I remember an America of nickel Cokes at the drugstore after school, when rock music blared from a flashing neon jukebox in the corner and Keith and Betty danced. Girls always turned their heads to watch us go by, when we cruised through town in Phil's two-tone red and white '57 Chevy. An oily shell of industrial prosperity protected America in those days; a naïve vision of earth framed in a free trade image. Free and easy for the temperate and hard working, TVs in every living room and 50-cent double feature movies on lazy Sunday afternoons.

Life is just a crap game and I am a player shooting my point. This pavement is hard and gray though; no empathy here, just chance, cold and crisp. White shadows tinge the landscape of a near-distant morning.

The moon is a silver cycle embedded in the tender side of the night like a nagging thorn that only time can suck out.

Winter ghosts and goblins lace the light, weaving me in.

Emotional philosophy peels dead skin from my brain in a slow painful itch.

Pastel sparks flash from my eyes' red sockets.

Feather wrenches turn twisted perceptions into shape.

Some kind of neo-geometry measures the impulses of bioelectrical insights revealed.

I love the way that roads complete cities, making them appear to be so clear and easy to navigate.

Sounds of morning phone lines ring and intersect with this room.

December passes in temptations of warm hearts.

Snowbirds seek mountain glides, unafraid of swooping abandon.

I love the way my cigarette smoke rolls and curls in the cold sun of this December smoking porch.

Frost forms like crystal smoke on the window.

The sun burns white spots through the frozen glass.

This early morning daydream is just another pinball ricochet into another video direction. Again and again, flippers flap and chrome balls roll back down the table, dancing to numb bell-beats they depend on the lightening reflexes of the player's dumb surrender to the physics of the machine.

Worlds of business and art blend and separate; then clash and smash into each other again, like the pastel molecules that hold this whole neon order together.

Mind missiles streak through the night, following coordinates to laser-guided centers of targets beneath basement shelters of crumbling buildings.

Flesh-stone secrets are whispered into mega-ton ears.

Unrest looms in the hunger of robot duties to perform.

Legions assemble and break through this snow-capped morning.

Ice starts fall from a smothered gray sky.

Zap-on moments of morning chill factors weigh on frosty windows.

Massive crowds of clouds whirl and stop, too low and stiff to pass over these mountains, and crisp trees standing at attention; like old soldiers stationed along the borders of this great white plane. A blast of ice wind ruptures the silence.

I am a one-legged dance instructor teaching a turtle how to float over a pond, instead of swimming through it.

I am the night manager of a day care center for kidnapped children who curse their mother's love.

I am a shipwrecked sailor searching for a piece of wreckage to float on.

I am a third basemen diving for hot grounders, hit by an octopus with eight bats.

I am a seasoned veteran of dance halls, paying fifty cents a dance for just one last chance at love.

JASON

1.

My daughter has a black and white photograph of Jason hanging on the wall of her bedroom. It is an image of a young boy wearing toy sunglasses with black rims; but the lenses of the glasses are missing, so his playful eyes are exposed. He is posing for the camera in a striped T-shirt, laughing into the eye of the lens. I have another photo of him in a small frame on top of my TV. He is a teenage boy leaning back on two legs in a kitchen chair at a friend's house. He is lanky and lean in a short-sleeved shirt. His hair is cut in a New York, New Wave style. His smile is wide and his shirt is unbuttoned, revealing a white T-skirt beneath. He is relaxing and goofing around with friends at a buddy's house.

I spread other photos of him on the kitchen table, stovetop and kitchen counters, then walk around the room and look at them. In some of the pictures, he is young and has a Prince Valiant haircut. In other pictures, his cherub face is round, soft and bright, like a full moon on a clear winter night. One of my favorite pictures is a close-up of him when he was about five or six years old. He is licking a huge vanilla ice-cream cone. The ice cream is smeared on and dripping from his lips, cheeks and chin. He has a very serious look on his face, like he means business with that cone.

In another image he is a young boy, seven or eight years old maybe, posing in a zip-up jump suit with a Flight Commander patch sewn onto the breast. His shoulders are small and his arms are folded, like he is hugging himself. In other pictures, he is an early teen on a ladder, painting our house, or a young boy clowning around at Silver

104

Lake, making goofy ears and eyes at the lens while sticking out his tongue.

I only have one photo of us together when he was young. He is sitting on my lap in a rocking chair in a pale yellow room. Sunlight is pouring through the door behind us in a white cone. We are framed in radiance. My favorite photo of him was taken one day when he was waiting in our Volkswagen mini-van at a pit stop during the summer of our New England migration. He looked ready to go, as if he heard the highway calling and was Bound for Glory like Woody Guthrie or Jack Kerouac; his curious bright eyes are wide open and fixed on the road.

2.

Jason had been missing for about four days; hiding out from the law for a crime he had committed the previous weekend. When he and his girlfriend broke into a neighbor's house to borrow a videotape while the neighbors were out of town. The neighbors were good friends of the family; and Jason and their son were the same age and friends at school. They freely entered each other's homes so Jason thought it would be okay. When the neighbors returned and found out about it though, they called the police. When Jason found out that the police were looking for him, he hid out. And all of his friends swore that they didn't know where he was.

I was working late at the shop, to get an order together that had to go out the next morning, when a city cop and a state trooper walked in. "May I help you?" I asked.

"Could we speak outside for a minute sir?"

"Sure." I said.

We stepped out and the trooper said, "We found Jason."

"That's great! Where is he? I wanna see 'im."

"We found his car parked in a quarry just north o' town." The trooper said. His eyes were clear and steady. "I'm sorry sir, but he's deceased." He said.

"What!? Whatta ya mean? How do you know?"

"We found his body in his car; and one end of a rubber hose was attached to the exhaust pipe, and the other end was duct-taped into the rear window. The car was out of gas. I'm sorry sir." He said.

An iron hammer pounded the walls of my chest. Blood rushed through my veins like mountain goats were head butting and bashing the inside walls of my chest. "Is there anything I can do?" the trooper asked.

"No. I'm okay. I'll work it out. I have to get home now though." I answered.

3.

It was a dull gray December day folding into the night. Jason drove to a quarry where he and his friends always hung out in the summertime for parties, beers and jokes; it was a personal place of power. He pulled into the gravel pit and turned off the car. He was cold but that make much difference. The heater in the car never work very well anyway and besides, his wet chill ran deep.

How white the moonlight is on the quarry walls against the black sky. He thought. *All of the other guys are gone and hellhounds are on my trail. It's nobody's fault but mine. It just worked out that way. This might be my new birth shock-conception of the white pleasure-pain of light. I am curious though; will my real name finally appear to me through all of this confusion?"*

He opened the door and climbed out to retrieve the death-tool that he had fashioned a few months earlier, in preparation for this night. A bitter wind blew. Flurrying snow swirled around his head as he attached one end of the tool to the exhaust pipe, and sealed the other end into the rear window with cardboard and duct tape. Then he climbed into the driver's seat, started the engine, settled back, closed his eyes and relaxed.

The smell isn't that bad, he thought, *and I hear that you get high and giddy on suffocation as the oxygen gets used up in your brain. The windows are fogging up, spreading from the edges to the center; enclosing me in mist. Soul mist pours from the top of my head like steam. I'm so tired. My thoughts rush out and all of the haunting voices are silenced at last. I feel so warm and gone."*

CAR WARS

Episode 1

I bought a used Chevy Impala from Chico, a friend from the Center Street Saloon. The Chevy had a few problems, but Chico told me what they were so I knew what I had to do to keep it going. One problem was that the windshield wasn't sealed very well, so water leaked in sometimes, when it rained. The day I drove it home, a slow leak in the right front tire went flat in the driveway overnight. It was a minor problem; except for the fact that the car had no jack in the trunk, and I had neglected to look for one. Chico didn't tell me that the car had no spare, and I never checked it out.

I called Chico and told him about it, and he brought his jack over. We fixed the tire and I was on the road again, but only for about a week. That's when the left ball joint broke as I was driving home from the store one night. When it broke, the car pulled sideways toward the ditch, about a quarter of a mile from my house. I managed to miss the ditch then wrestled the car home and into my driveway. When I got out and checked its broken foot, I decided that the merciful thing to do was shoot the Chevy and put us both out of our misery. I had no money to buy another car though. I had to fix it. The problem was, I was not very mechanical. Fixing machines never interested me, so I didn't know what to do or how to do it. I didn't even have the proper tools I needed to complete the job.

Fortunately, I had recently purchased a 1980 Ford F-100 pick-up truck; all I had to do was register it with the department of motor vehicles in Montpelier and I'd have wheels again. The truck was a worn-out beauty; six cylinders, easy on gas, just up from Florida with only 70,000 miles on the odometer. The body suffered from a little surface rust but was basically ready for the road. When I tried to register it though, I found out that a vehicle from out of state had to be checked out by a cop, I.D. number, Bill of Sale, etc., and could only be registered at the Department of Motor Vehicles in Montpelier; a trip I could easily make in about half a day, if I had a car. So, I returned to plan A, not shooting the Chevy but fixing it, without any of the required tools or knowledge I needed to complete the job. The Chevy was jacked-up and falling apart in the driveway. If I could just get it running, at least temporarily, I could drive to Montpelier and register the truck. I'd have two cars then and my transportation problems would be over.

I worked on the Chevy for about a week, but still couldn't fix it; so I borrowed Michael's car and drove to Montpelier to register the truck. Michael couldn't drive; due to a recent back operation, so she said I could use her car for as long as I wanted. I drove her big-boat Olds around for a week or so and forgot about registering the truck, as I continued to work on the Chevy. The Olds was in pretty rough shape itself. Water leaked in from the top of the windshield when it rained, and the headlights and turn signals didn't always work; but I could drive it on clear days. I agreed to fix these problems for her, in exchange for using the car. Another week passed and the Chevy was still down. So, Lyn and Sibyl took the Olds to the grocery store one night, bought about six bags of groceries and headed home. On the way back, they were caught in a thunderstorm. Rain leaked through the top of the windshield, dripped down the inside of the glass to the dashboard and shorted out the headlights.

Lyn was driving blind on a black, rain drenched country road. She steered the car into the driveway of a farmhouse along the way, knocked on the door and asked the folks who lived there if she could use their phone to call me to pick them up, along with the food, in the illegal truck. It was a good idea but I was on the phone with my friend, Chicago Frank, when she called. Frank and I didn't get to talk much, so, when we got the chance, we talked for long periods of time. That night, we talked for over an hour. Lyn kept calling but couldn't get through. The man of the house finally got tired of waiting and drove Lyn and Sibyl home, along with all of the groceries. When they dripped into the kitchen with the wet sagging bags of food, I was still on the phone. Lyn slouched through the door like a wet cat crawling in from the storm. I looked at her, said good-bye to Frank and hung up.

"What happened?" I asked, and she told me about the rain, the headlights and black road; and the broken car parked in the farmer's driveway that had to be picked up in the morning. I walked down to the farm and drove the car back next morning. I could drive it during the day, but not at night. The day after that, I drove to Montpelier in the Old's and registered the truck.

Episode II.

The truck's down now. I can't get it inspected. There are holes in the floor that need to be patched, the muffler is rotten and the license plate is wired on in the wrong place and not illuminated. I was going to New York in the morning, to work on some fat cat's swimming pool for cash; but now I have to spend some money instead, although I need the money from the job to pay for the parts I need to fix the truck.

110

I work all afternoon and into the night. It takes four trips to the auto-parts store, two bashed and bleeding knuckles, three sections of bent and cumbersome exhaust pipes of different sizes, with inserts and extensions, hammers pounding, cold chisels, grinding metal, fiber glass fabrication; a self grounding light for the back plate and the truck is on the road again.

Episode III.

Lyn and I stop for gas. We don't have any cash, but we have a credit card. The gas tank on the Chevy has a hole in the top though, so we can only fill the tank halfway. We pull into the station and Lyn says, "Ten dollars please." But the attendant misunderstands and fills the tank, while Lyn and I are engaged in our conversation. Gas leaks onto the road as we drive, gushing at first. Lyn doesn't say anything. There's nothing much to say. She signs the slip, fires the Chevy up and we head home, a Molotov cocktail on wheels. I hope no one drops a cigarette.

THE WAVE

    I was caught in a wild wave off the coast of Cape Cod on a mid-August afternoon. My family and I had rented a campsite outside of Provincetown. The sky was crystal blue and the sun was a great white disk floating in wispy clouds. A hurricane was raging off of the coast of Florida, churning the Atlantic all the way up the coast. I was sitting on the beach in the clean white sand, watching my kids play in the seething waves that smashed the land and sun the tanned tourists. Two great breakers rose and rolled onto the shore like synchronized twins, one right behind the other; hurling thousands of gallons of ocean that slapped the beach. I wanted to bodysurf, riding those slingshot waves and sliding across the beach on my chest to a skidding stop on my blanket, laughing in the smooth heat. I wanted to meld with the salt of that mad water, so I waded in and Lyn said, "Where're ya goin'?"

"For a swim. Ya wanna come?" I said.

"Not me, I'm not goin' out there!"

"It'll be okay. See those people swimmin' between the waves? All we gotta do is get through that first breaker wall and It'll be fine. Come on!"

"No way!" she said. So I worked my way to the nearest breaker and was immediately swept off of my feet. I plunged headfirst through the boiling wall of water and into the calm shallow water that shifted between the two breakers. I drifted, played and body surfed in the farthest wave; my body jutting out like a hood ornament attached to the nose of that, '54 V-8 Buick, Duo-Glide mountain of water. I would rise in the wave and rush toward the shore, then stop before I reached

112

the first breaker wall. I rode between the two waves, until I was too tired to ride anymore and headed back in.

When I reached the back of the closest breaker that separated me from the beach; the smooth swell of the wave seemed calm, but it concealed the foaming turbulence of the other side, so I dove right in. The wave wrapped me in its crashing current, like a great Wave God gripping me in its watery fist. I was helpless, alone and at His mercy. He spun me around and upside down, and any other way his wild will desired. His thundering laughter filled my senses with liquid vibrations that were too loud to hear with my ears alone. I didn't even know which way was up, and was unable to get there anyway, unless the wave god willed it. *Will my breath last?* I thought. *Where is the sky? Empty your lungs and fill them again, when your head pops up, before you are snatched back under again.* Splashing visions of being washed out to sea flashed through my mind. I tumbled over and over again, until I was thrown onto the shore with all of the other sea-debris sand and seaweed, driftwood and stones, small fish and carcasses of fish, the seashell remains of an infinite seafood feast of the Atlantic's liquid history. I landed face down on the sand, floundering on the shore. Dozens of sun-pink tourists splashed ankle deep in the white froth of the wave finishing around me. Then I crawled from the water, like the first fish that ever crawled onto land, scraping my tender fins, gills and scaly under-belly on the jagged rocks and sand.

When I gathered my strength, I stood up and walked across the beach in a daze; then fell face first onto my towel. Lyn and the kids were wading in the surf. A little later, when my fear and pain evaporated in the sun, and my sea-scales flaked away; I felt like the first-fish that ever crawled from the water onto the land, on that first amphibian day, then lingered on the beach a while longer, before slipping back into the sea.

PHOENIX

Arizona is dry, brown and bristly; these desert plants are so exotic, compared to the snow covered pines back home. I am visiting my dad. I haven't seen him since he and my mom divorced, and he moved out here with his girlfriend, Vi, who he met in a bowling alley bar in Ohio on a league night. I drive them to a casino on an Indian reservation north of town. Dad can't drive; he's seventy-eight and his stroke and heart condition prevent it. Vi can't drive either, so I get the job. The temperature is in the high 80's or low 90's and the further we drive the more the city blends with the desert. Sandy plains spread to tan mountains in the distance. Huge piles of brown earth look like great golden bears sleeping in the sun, under a cloudless sky stretching to the shimmering horizon. There are wrinkles in the bears' pelts, where the hot-wind has gouged and baked the sand. The road is an arrow through a reservation land that white men don't need, so they granted it to the natives in pale-faced compassion.

"Everyone has to be somewhere," the white-eyes say, "but we'll keep the best. You can live here." The natives fooled the white-eyes though. They put a casino in the middle of the reservation; so all of the white folks would come to drink firewater, gamble, and donate money to the tribe.

On the way to the casino, we pass a huge housing development stuck in the middle of the reservation. Palm trees line the streets of an oasis-suburbia built on the generosity of white-eyed greed. I imagine the tribal council laughing about it in a luxurious conference room behind the complex. Dad and Vi give the tribe some money too, but they laugh about it. "Just lookin' for a good time." Dad says, "It's just play money anyway, ya can't take it with ya. I'm just tryin' ta win, knowin' that even if I do, I'll keep playin' 'til I lose." He laughs.

We drive for about forty minutes to Harrah's Casino, a tribal, Las Vegas style enterprise on outside of a one-light reservation town in the middle of nowhere. There's a fountain in front of the place. Carved stone statues of Native Americans perform daily chores, hunting or grinding corn. A valet takes the car. He wears a white shirt and black vest with delicate beaded designs. Dad, Vi and I walk through the door. A neon hum of activity greets us. Lights flash and blink, bells ring, fortune seekers crowd colorful spinning machines; feeding and dispensing tokens; and winning, sometimes to keep them interested. I don't gamble. It doesn't interest me. Dad and Vi love it. They play ten to twenty bucks at a time. Waitresses deliver drinks to mobs of customers jamming buckets of coins into the slots. They have everything here, one-armed bandits, crap-games, card games, Bingo and Keno. Dad and Vi play a few of the machines then head for the bar. They can gamble there too, on slot machines that poke up in front of each laid back, padded stool.

There's a stage behind the bar, about head high to the bartenders. A cowboy band plays for Dad and Vi; and all of the other good ol' boys and gals, seniors now, dancin' country-style in the southwest afternoon. These guys can really play. They know all the old songs, from Hank Williams to Mel Tillis. They are dressed in cowboy hats, shirts and jeans, taking turns with the songs they know best; each piece, a favorite bar-ballad or lost wedding-ring song of lonesome despair. Dad rocks in his stool and sings along. The band is younger than the audience, but between sets they mingle with the seniors, drink at their tables, talk with them and laugh.

116

Dad and Vi punch slot machine buttons and drink short drafts all afternoon. I watch them for a while, then wander around the place to watch the other gamblers work. Then I buy a few souvenirs for back home, and a cap for me. I have been thinking about getting a cowboy hat though, since first I heard that band. I have a mid-afternoon chili dog for lunch, then head back to the bar. I order a draft and sit at a small empty table. A man in a wheel chair rolls up next to me and asks me to get him a beer. I do. We talk. He says, "I'm just here for the music."

"I know watcha mean." I reply. Then we sit back, sip our beers as we listen to the band. A young, thin blond waitress, with long legs in a short skirt, keeps passing our table and glancing my way; smiling glittering brown eyes in my direction, looking for a good tip maybe. It feels good to be noticed by a pretty young girl though. It dosen't happen much any more.

Dad is ahead of the game most of the day, but keeps playing until he loses. Vi's almost a thousand dollars up, but she keeps playing until she loses too. When we leave, they tell jokes about all of the money they lost. The valet brings the car around, Dad tips him and we drive back to Phoenix. The desert highway shimmers ahead of us and I laugh at their stories of losing all of the way home.

CHICAGO FRANK

I met Frank in little league baseball. We didn't play on the same team, he was two years younger than I was, but he lived next door to the ball-field and hung around at all the practices and games. We always found something to do or talk about, and became good friends. We lost touch after high school, and I didn't see Frank again for about ten years. I was just finishing college, and he was undesirably discharged from the Coast Guard for refusing to follow orders. He told me sailor stories and gave me copies of *Zen Flesh, Zen Bones* and *The Journal of Albion Moonlight* to read. He had become a musician, leather-working, poet-philosopher in a bread truck van. He worked in a candle factory on the midnight shift; eating speed beans and pouring hot wax onto steel tables with half dollar size holes drilled in them, to capture and mold the beeswax into light.

Frank drove an old bread-truck van that he wanted to sell, so he painted "FOR SALE $500" signs on both sides along with his telephone number. We stole about twenty baskets of peaches from a local grocery store in that van one night. The parking lot of the store was well lit-up like a fluorescent day. The owners believed that the lights would be enough to keep the bandits away, so they left the peaches out front. Frank drove right in though, advertising how he could be reached, and we jumped out and loaded the van; then took the peaches back to my house. My wife freaked out. Baskets of peaches covered our kitchen floor; and we ate peach pie and cobbler for weeks.

Later, Frank drove big rig trucks, and restored old Indian and Harley Davidson motorcycles with his dad. They even created a little museum of classic bikes. Frank looked like a cross between a Hell's

Angel and a blues-harp player from the south side of Chicago. He had a goatee and wore a black leather jacket. He wore small wire rimmed glasses that he glared through like an anarchist from an old Russian novel. When he moved to Rutland, he rolled into town on a classic white and chrome Harley-Davidson "Hog", late fifties or early sixties maybe; sleek, heavy, wide and throaty, highway duo-glide. He was heavier than I remembered. "I'm Nationwide!" he said. He walked with a limp because one leg was shorter than the other; due to a motorcycle accident followed by hospital bedtime, operations and recoveries on Bourbon, painkillers and beer.

On Frank's first night in town, Lyn and I met him at the Back Home Café, after an Amnesty International lecture we attended. Lyn had befriended a young German boy at the lecture and invited him to join us. He was a blond-haired, blue-eyed Aryan youth representative for the organization. We met Frank after the lecture and sat on the deck of the Cafe. Frank bought pitchers of Kamikazes; and when the pitchers were empty, he'd throw the left over ice in the pitcher into the air and call for another. The German kid joined right in. Neal joined us too, along with Gary and Chris.

The German boy was flirting with the hottest waitress in the place all night; making eyes at her and she was making eyes back. They danced during her breaks, fast and slow, embracing cheek-to-cheek. She had her arms around his neck when we left; and he had her pinned against the wall as he kissed her. Their writhing tongues seemed to be seeking entrance to each other's souls. Frank drove the boy home on his Harley, when the bar closed and we followed. The boy grinned through the summer night-wind sweeping his face. The band had asked Frank to play harmonica with them that night. Frank always talked to musicians who were playing in bars, and they always invited him to join them at some point during the show.

I visited Frank and Buda, his wife, a few years later. They were living in a suburb of Cleveland. Buda was a silversmith who had a classic collection of switchblades. They had two sons. Frank drove an oil truck for a living. A professor friend of mine was giving a reading, and speaking at Cleveland State University while we were there. Frank and I went to the reading, but Frank couldn't stand the academic atmosphere of the place, so we headed to a bar in The Flats of Cleveland. We drank short drafts and shots of Peach Schnapps with the bartender all afternoon. That night, we drove into town to hear Hollywood Slim, a blues band that was playing in a club downtown. Frank and Slim talked between sets and during the third set, Slim walked over and handed the microphone and harp to Frank in the middle of a song, and Frank blew his heart out to the crowd.

I didn't see Frank again for about five years, but we kept in close phone contact. He stopped drinking and drugging, bought a semi-rig and hired out for long distance runs. We just missed him, when we passed through Cleveland on the way home from our cross-country trip. He was on a three-day run to Michigan. I called him about a year later, but he wasn't home. Buda said. "Frank fell off a ladder and hurt his back a couple of years ago, and after that he got hooked on painkillers in the hospital. When he came home, he kept eatin' those and chasin' 'em down with whisky an' beer. Then he moved onto heroin an' lost the truck to the bank, so I filed for divorce. He moved out about a year ago, and I haven't seen him or heard from him since."

Buda called again last night, "Frank's dead." She said. "I thought you would want to know."

"Wadda ya mean! Whadda ya talkin' about! How? Why? Where? When?"

"He had a heart attack from a heroin overdose." She said. "We were just gettin' back together, and I'd heard from a mutual friend that he was in bad shape. She told me the name of the street where he lived, but she didn't know the address, so I drove around the neighborhood to find him an' bring 'im home. I knew it was his place when I drove by and saw the beautiful lace curtains and decorations hangin' in the window. I parked the car, walked to the door and knocked. He answered and let me in. We talked and I convinced him to come home.

He'd been home for about a month or so, and was in rehab. He was workin' again. He even took one of the boys with him on an overnight run to Indiana. We were talkin' again. Then, my grandmother in West Virginia got sick and I had to leave to take care of her. While I was gone, he hooked up with some old drug buddies. A stranger found his body in the parkin' lot. I didn't know he was dead until I got home."

NO EXIT

My family and I camped in the White Mountain National Forest of New Hampshire last weekend with Neal and his son, Justin. I had camped in that area years before, in a campground near a small mountain town. The campground was owned by The Fahey Motel, which was located on the bank of the Swift River roaring between the winding mountain highway, white cliffs and towering trees.

John Fahey was one of my favorite musicians. He was a guitar player who developed a pure mystical-American folk sound of hypnotic rhythms that tickled my soul. My friend, John Campy, turned me onto Fahey one night when he brought an album over. The album was called *The Transfiguration of Blind Joe Death*. On the cover of the album was a pen and ink drawing of a black blues man in a white turban, and a long white robe with flared sleeves. He sat cross-legged with a guitar lying on his lap, as he contemplated an old black, blind angel-man with a cane perched on one arm; and a bare breasted falcon-woman with black shoulder-length hair, draped across her face, hooked on the other arm. Jungle foliage filled the nighttime background. Animals gathered behind and around the blues man in the underbrush. The border of the drawing was pale green with skeletons sketched in white. Fahey's twelve-string guitar's whining slides of a thousand steel notes somehow sounded just like the picture. "What kinda music is this?" I asked.

"Well," Campy said, "Fahey was just a blues guitar picker who went fishin' and never came back." So, when I saw the Fahey Motel nestled on the bank of that little river, I imagined that John Fahey had gone fishing there and was never heard from again. He bought a little motel and sheltered wandering tourists as he fished and picked the blue guitar days away in the cool mountain sun.

We headed to Whales Tail Water Park the next day. The park was a concrete aqua-playground nestled in the White Mountains. There were three giant pools for swimming, and a wave machine. We floated on inner tubes down a lazy river that flowed through the park. We slid down water slides of all shapes and sizes. The kids were laughing and wet all day, and running in the sun. Finally, I gathered enough courage to ride the biggest curling slide in the park. The first trip down took my breath away as I careened through tubes and around wild curves. In some places, large sections of the ceiling had been removed and I slid right up to the edge of the sky; convinced each time that I was going over. When I reached the bottom though, my heart was racing and I was charged on reckless energy. So I rode the thrill-slide again and again, addicted to the danger play of gravity and water.

Later in the afternoon, Neal and I lounged in deck chairs, soaking up the sun. I was staring at the entrance of the park as crowds of water world adventurers lined up to leave. A sign above a set of unopened gates said, NO EXIT, as families waited to squeeze through the only two gates that were open. *Why don't they open those other gates?* I thought. *It would be a lot easier for folks to leave that way.*

I made a new friend in my martial arts class. His name is Guy. He is a little overweight but flexible, alert and quick, and handles himself pretty well. He reads interesting books. We have had wonderful conversations about Kierkegaard, Sartre, Camus, Thomas Wolfe, and James Joyce. In the locker room the other night, changing for class, I told Guy about a Jack Spicer poem I had read and a line that I liked in particular, "Hell is where we place ourselves when we wish to look up."

Guy said, "Hell is other people."

"Where'd ya hear that?" I asked.

"A Sartre play called *No Exit*," he said. "I'll see ya upstairs."

I was drinking my morning coffee and listening to the radio when a news flash came on. The announcer said that Guy had been arrested in Connecticut for beating his parents to death. *They must be talkin' about another Guy,* I thought, but no, it was my Guy. It was like all those other news stories of sudden assassins that you hear about; when all of their friends and neighbors all say, "I don't understand, he was so quiet. He never bothered anyone or caused any trouble. He was a real gentleman, a real nice guy." Then, for some reason, the guy snaps and kills some people. After that, the authorities either arrest him or shoot him, or he shoots himself, and it's all over.

The reporter said that Guy had been institutionalized for mental problems for a while, but had recently been living successfully on his own. He had visited his parents in Connecticut, the previous weekend, to borrow some money from them for a trip out west. They refused to give it to him though, so Guy went into rage. He kicked them, punched them and beat them with anything he could get his hands on; a stool, a vase and part of a banister he ripped from the staircase. The authorities even found Guy's bloody footprints on his dead mother's back, where he had apparently jumped on her while she was lying face down in her own gore. The bodies were so badly mutilated that the authorities had to consult dental records for positive IDs.

www.ingramcontent.com/pod-product-compliance
Lightning Source LLC
Chambersburg PA
CBHW050802250626
47155CB00005B/2173